ADVANCE PRAISE FOR
THE REGISTRY OF FORGOTTEN OBJECTS

"*The Registry of Forgotten Objects* is impressive for the unique and inventive vision of the author. These stories consider the permanence that abides beneath the surface of all that leaves this world and the desire to believe that 'everything is part of a pattern, everything rises.' No truer words could be said about this collection. Miles Harvey is a masterful storyteller." —Lee Martin

"This astonishingly beautiful book of interlocking stories has at its center things and people that are about to disappear. Sometimes what has been lost, however, can be recovered. It is as if all these stories compose one large story, an emotional journey of the lost and found. It should be read from beginning to end—people and things, such as a barber pole, migrate from one story to another. A wonderful book." —Charles Baxter

"Like a magician pulling a rabbit from a hat, Miles Harvey plucks mysterious coins from cobblestones, a sphere from the sea, a dusty postcard from a not-quite-empty house. In this beautiful collection, both lives and objects glow, with the light and weight of choices and longings that echo across stories, relationships, years." —Caitlin Horrocks

"*The Registry of Forgotten Objects* sated an appetite I hadn't realized I had. Harvey's fable-like stories conjure a world full of doors and subtle connections, a place both familiar and endlessly surprising. In our uncertain times, this book offers a powerful and necessary reminder that not only fear but also beauty resides in what is strange and unknown. This linked collection is masterful—one I'll return to again and again." —V. V. Ganeshanantha

T0283730

THE REGISTRY OF FORGOTTEN OBJECTS

THE JOURNAL NON/FICTION PRIZE

THE REGISTRY OF FORGOTTEN OBJECTS

Stories

Miles Harvey

MAD CREEK BOOKS, AN IMPRINT OF
THE OHIO STATE UNIVERSITY PRESS
COLUMBUS

Published by Mad Creek Books, an imprint of The Ohio State University Press.

Library of Congress Cataloging-in-Publication Data
Names: Harvey, Miles, 1960– author.
Title: The registry of forgotten objects : stories / Miles Harvey.
Other titles: Registry of forgotten objects (Compilation)
Description: Columbus : Mad Creek Books, an imprint of The Ohio State
    University Press, [2024] | Summary: "Short stories that use inanimate
    objects and how humans relate to them to examine grief, environmental
    disaster, and other themes of contemporary life"—Provided by publisher.
Identifiers: L CCN 2 024009637 | I SBN 9 780814259146 (paperback) |
    ISBN 0814259146 (paperback) | ISBN 9780814283615 (ebook) | ISBN
    0814283616 (ebook)
Subjects: LCGFT: Short stories.
Classification: L CC P S3608.A78918 R 44 2 024 | D DC 8 13/.6—dc23/eng/
    20240509
LC record available at https://lccn.loc.gov/2024009637

Cover design by Nathan Putens
Text design by Juliet Williams
Type set in Sabon

For Scott Blackwood and Doro Boehme

Returning memories?
No, at the time of death
I'd like to see lost objects
return instead.

—WISŁAWA SZYMBORSKA

CONTENTS

THE DROUGHT

I

On the fourth month of the second year of the drought which brought so much despair to our community, the weatherman began to grow his beard. Inconsequential as it might seem to the rest of the world, no event in the annals of our town has been more contentious—except, of course, for the weatherman's disappearance. To his followers, whose zeal has only grown since his abrupt departure from our midst, the beard is a symbol of his courage, his commitment to his fellow man, his compassion for the suffering of others during those terrible times. His detractors, some of them equally fanatical, regard those same whiskers as the ultimate affectation of a dangerous demagogue. Other townspeople, meanwhile, look back on that day's faint stubble as the first sign of madness. Theories regarding his motivation for the beard increase with time. It is said that he joined a religious sect or that he hoped to hide a facial rash or that he was inspired by a dream of nine whiskered men swimming in a sparkling turquoise sea. The truth, however, is less dramatic: the weatherman forgot to shave. On that fateful day, he arrived at the television studio just moments before his portion of the morning news, having spent the night in a dusty pasture at the edge of town with the wife of a local barber, their skin resplendent with moonglow, the withered grass silvered and shimmering, as if given new life by the night.

II

It is not easy to keep a secret in a community such as ours. Although it boasts one hundred thousand residents, two television stations, a regional airport, a convention center, a four-year college, an art museum, a new esplanade along the river, and a handful of buildings tall enough to be described as skyscrapers, the place still harbors the soul of a small town. It began as a trading post, grew into a fort, then a railway junction, then a stockyards, and became a city only because people needed a place in which to shop and eat and worship and love on this little-populated expanse of high plains. We may have our own cineplexes and gourmet coffee shops, but we cannot offer the only urban amenity that matters: true privacy. Anyone wandering the bars on Center Street, for instance, is likely to happen upon several old friends, a few business associates, the occasional third cousin, and, on a bad night, an ex-spouse or two. Those who require anonymity usually retreat to some isolated rural compound or move to a real city.

But even now, the town knows nothing of the weatherman and the barber's wife, a secret all the more astounding for the fact that it was more or less kept by accident. True, they shunned all the usual trappings of illicit romance—no clandestine interludes in neon-lit motels or windowless restaurants, no hand-holding under tables or rushed embraces at parties or back doors left unlocked. But this had less to do with precaution than the operatic nature of their passion. Their meeting places were as primal and expansive as their attraction to one another. Morning and night, the weatherman would go before the cameras to report that a stalled high-pressure system still haunted us, that the heat wave continued to shatter records, that no end to the drought was in sight. Then, following the ten o'clock news, he would climb in his car and race into the windswept outlands, the road before him vanishing now and again beneath clouds of dust. Our city has never been difficult to escape: from an airplane at night, it looks like a small island of light amid a great sea of darkness. The drought, moreover, had further emptied the countryside. Farms lay in ruin, and countless local businesses, many of which had been in the same family for generations, closed their doors. It was behind one such building, a shuttered gas station at a rural crossroads, that the weatherman would park his car, then lean against the cinder block wall and wait for the sound of her pickup truck, its loose manifold raging beneath the hood, soft blue-grass music floating from the cab. She barely seemed to brake, slowing down just enough for him to open the door and lunge inside before they roared off in search of some devastated land-scape to share. They made love in parched fields between rows of stunted corn. They made love in wasted orchards, withered apples dropping softly on their backs. They made love on soil so dry their naked limbs dangled into huge fissures baked open in the earth.

I do not know when the weatherman began venturing across the street from the TV studio to the little salon the woman and her husband owned on River Road. What I can say for certain is that he was not the first man (or woman) who patronized that shop simply to be in her presence. She was not an out-going or a friendly person, and even before I knew anything about her, I sensed that she was deeply unhappy. Yes, she was beautiful—lush head of harvest-wheat hair, seductive smile that trembled between melancholic and malevolent, delicate face spared from bland perfection by an asymmetry that seemed to project two expressions at once—but that was only part of her allure. When cutting hair, she stood erect, her chin raised, her slim torso motionless but her arms ablur, the scissors snapping in syncopated rhythms that settled in your mind like melodies. She eschewed small talk, uttering barely a word between *Have a seat* and *All done.* Sometimes, she seemed to lapse into a kind of daydream, her eyes fixed on an object against the wall or closed entirely, as though her hands had an intelligence of their own. You could almost believe some invisible force flowed from those long fingers, penetrating your scalp, pulsing down your spine, unknotting your pains, emptying your thoughts. Strange as it may sound, you never left her chair without feeling utterly revitalized, as if the talc she dusted on your neck, its fragrance lingering in your nostrils, was part of some enchantment.

Still, it surprised me to learn that the weatherman had fallen into her company. I had seen him with several women before, all of them handsome and exotic, all of them from back east. They would fly in for weekends, wearing sunglasses and smirks, and when perfunctory introductions were required, those women would nod at us like worthies greeting the peasantry. They did not bother to remember our names, nor we theirs: their place in the weatherman's life was as tenuous as our own. A naturally charismatic man with bemused blue eyes, he gave the impression of someone who might have been a movie star or congressman had he not chosen a career in meteorology. I'm still not certain what drew him to that line of work. He told me that science had interested him barely more than other subjects during a childhood devoted to skateboarding instead of scholarship. The son of a Lutheran minister, he had been groomed to follow his father into divinity school, but after an undergraduate degree in religious studies, he broke from the path laid out for him, drifting through a succession of jobs—bodyguard, ski instructor, luxury-car salesman—before entering a master's program in meteorology during his late twenties. When I asked him about the leap from Christianity to climatology, he was typically evasive. *I sometimes think,* he said, flashing that inscrutable grin of his, *that knowing the weather is as close as you can get to knowing God.*

In retrospect, those words seem like a warning, but at the time I assumed it was just another one of his jokes. Those days, the only thing he seemed to take seriously was his work, spending hours poring over Doppler radar data and satellite imagery and National Weather Service maps. He had big plans, making it clear from the start that his stay in our midst would be temporary. Forging few real friendships in town, even among his coworkers, he attended social functions only when professional duty required it. The furniture in his apartment was rented, the lease month to month. Until the barber's wife, he had professed a complete indifference to local women.

Therefore, the weatherman told me, it was unnerving for him to discover that in some perverse way, he desired her precisely because she seemed so native to the soil. The smell of the dust was the smell of her skin. He came to believe that she embodied the whole spirit of the town: its toughness, its inwardness, its air of frustration and gloom. Her only child, a four-year-old boy, had died in a horrible accident during the early months of the drought, when wildfires ravaged so much of the countryside they began to seem almost commonplace. One bright, blustery Sunday, as the barber drove his family home from a camping trip, feathers of smoke began to float across the interstate. The barber's wife wanted to pull off the road, but her husband refused. In his salon, the barber was an obsequious glad-hander; in his home, he was sullen and withdrawn; in his car, however, he was a sadist, karate-kicking the brake, ripping and clawing at the stick shift, throttling the wheel as if he wanted to twist it into a knot. They came out of a long curve, the prairie in front of them smoldering but only a few small patches of fire skittering amid the grass. Then, just as they approached, the wind shifted and the flames lurched and the highway disappeared in gray. Later, she could not recall the sound of the crash, only the truck's brake lights exploding from the vapor like a pair of huge crimson eyes. The barber managed to stagger away from the car, but his wife, pinned in the wreckage for two hours with her son, whom she could neither see nor touch, was forced to endure the boy's screams and then his silence, as she watched the prairie burn. The tragedy left her full of strange ideas. She said she despised the barber for what happened to their child. She said she could never leave the barber, whom she'd known all her life. She said the weatherman meant nothing to her. She said she was fated to be with the weatherman. She said that what the two of them did amid that dust was an act of salvation. She once whispered that they alone, through their passion, could bring life back to the land.

He worried for her sanity at such moments. How could he not? Yet, some moonless nights as he lay over her, his shadow obscuring all but the faint glint of her eyes, he had the feeling, horrible and magnificent, that he was thrusting himself directly into the earth.

III

It was I, the station manager, who insisted the weatherman allow his beard to grow. I am not a particularly brilliant or enterprising man: when I took this job, I accepted the fact that I had probably reached the pinnacle of my career. Never one to fit in easily, I had drifted in and out of three marriages and half a dozen mid-market cities before coming here in my early fifties. It is not the sort of place an outsider can fall in love with, but from the start I felt a particular affinity for it, this town of lost opportunities and frustrated dreams. Any success I've had comes from my inherent understanding of the local psyche, and as I stared at the weatherman's stubbled face on the monitor that first morning, I knew that those whiskers were a godsend. By that time, he was already a local celebrity—the leading expert on the drought and perhaps the most trusted man in town. He was blessed with one of those faces that is transfigured by television. In person, his appearance was somewhat gaunt, even frail, his natural expression one of apparent indifference. The camera seemed to transfuse him with blood and bones, purpose, and passion. Although he tended to avoid the eyes of others in conversation, his gaze, when metamorphosed by the airwaves, was so intense you almost felt he could see into your living room, so tender you wanted to believe he would hear you speak. In a time of monumental dread and uncertainty, the weatherman presented an aura of unwavering calm, empathy, and confidence. With the beard, however, he changed from a familiar face into a phenomenon—and eventually, in the minds of many, a prophet.

When I came to this station, the news programming ranked far behind our only competitor. I made it my mission to change that, but for years my efforts were met with frustration. Trying to recruit talent for the second-rate news operation in a prairie town is no easy task, and I admit to hiring more than my share of over-the-hill anchors who hide bottles of gin in the bathroom and pimply local boys who think it's clever to interrupt a sports report with birthday greetings to their former fraternity brothers. Every once in a while, however, I manage to stumble upon a diamond in the rough, a candidate with genuine talent who, for lack of training or connections or luck, might be desperate enough to endure exile in our town as a stepping stone to better opportunities. The weatherman had no previous professional experience before I found him; his audition tape was amateurish, his work history spotty, his grades mediocre. Yet I sensed from the start there was something special about him. I flew him out for an interview, tested him in front of the cameras, and offered him a job on the spot. He turned me down, saying that he expected interest from other stations, and, to be honest, that this one was far from his first choice. Three weeks later, however, he called back, completely unembarrassed, to inquire whether the position was still open. I had just made an offer to someone else but immediately rescinded it—a move of questionable ethics, perhaps, though one I have never regretted. A month after the weatherman's arrival, the market share of our 6:00 p.m. news had improved from a paltry thirteen to a respectable twenty. With the onset of the drought, our ratings boost was even more dramatic. By the end of that first year without rain—during which the weatherman, accepting my offer of doubled pay, had begun to work both the morning and evening shifts—viewership of our news programming had edged within a few points of the competition. Then came the beard. I had sensed it would give the weatherman the rough-and-ready look of a war correspondent, which, I reasoned, might strike a sympathetic chord with our beleaguered citizenry. But even I was unprepared for the magnitude of the response. Within weeks, we had established a solid lead on our rival. Ad revenues, despite the wretched state of the local economy, skyrocketed. Our corporate headquarters sent kudos, wall plaques, and bonuses. After years of complacency and self-doubt, I began, briefly, to entertain the idea of seeking work in a larger market.

My greatest fear was that the weatherman would leave before me. Each time he tramped into my office, I half expected him to announce his resignation, and whenever the phone rang, I wondered if it would be some other station checking his references. He had always insisted he would stay no longer than two years, but by the time his second anniversary at the station came and went, he had begun to develop an interest in the drought that, from its earliest manifestations, bordered on the fanatical. Immersing himself in history books, he would spend hours recounting details of such catastrophes: a famine in northern China, brought on by the failure of monsoon rains, that killed 9.5 million people in the late nineteenth century; a seven-hundred-year drought that wiped out an entire civilization in the Indus Valley beginning around 1800 BCE; a worldwide environmental meltdown, possibly triggered by the eruption of a volcanic isle in the Indian Ocean, that caused droughts from Mexico to Mongolia in the sixth century CE. He talked endlessly about the enigmatic weather event behind our own drought—a cooling of waters in the tropical Pacific, which, the weatherman explained, had pushed the jet stream northward, creating a stalled high-pressure area over our part of the world. La Niña, such an occurrence is called—"the girl." I became so accustomed to hearing that phrase roll off the weatherman's tongue that it barely surprised me when he began using it to refer to the barber's wife.

So it was, each in his own way, that the weatherman and I came to love the drought. Perhaps this unspoken and unspeakable bond, which set us so much at odds with the rest of the community, accounts for why he took me into his confidence. Or perhaps he simply concluded that I could keep a secret. If so, his trust was well placed, for no one else in town has ever known this story—or rather, I should say, no one but the barber. That unfortunate man was all too well aware of his wife's infidelity: she made no attempt to hide it from him. Why he chose to keep quiet about it remains unclear, though I suspect it had much to do with pride. She was nineteen when they married; he was thirty-four. I imagine that, with his custom-painted cars and gaudy cologne and bartender friends who poured round after round of free drinks, he seemed quite worldly to her back then. It must not have taken her more than a few years, however, to realize that her husband was as small as the town itself, a man whose dreams did not extend a block beyond the barbershop. Before his eyes, meanwhile, she must have undergone an equally alarming transformation, from a lightsome girl on whose beautiful body he could hang his choice of clothes and in whose eager mind he could impose his prejudices, to a complex and discontented woman whose intelligence and talents far exceeded his own. Prior to her arrival on the scene, for example, the barber had advertised his place of business with a gaudy plastic sign featuring his name in the same hand-painted lettering found on placards for the hot-dog stand down the street and the taqueria around the corner. She immediately made sure that eyesore was taken down, but instead of replacing it with a different sign, she devised a window display that looked like something out of a high-end day spa in a real city. Purchasing an old wooden barber pole at an auction, she hung it in front of a black background in the window and lit it in such a way that it appeared to be floating in mid-air. With that one bit of wordless branding, she began to transform the place from a sleepy, second-rate hair salon into a fashionable boutique, frequented by the sort of people who pass as trendsetters in this provincial metropolis.

The barber could not have failed to understand that this success was almost entirely due to her skill, industry, and allure, and while he no doubt despised her for it, he also must have feared what would become of him if they ever parted. Then, too, there was the prospect of public humiliation, no small terror for a vain and resentful man whose strongest claim

upon the world was possessing what others desired. Or perhaps he was simply paralyzed by guilt over the death of their
child. Whatever the case, when faced with the affair, he did not
act. An autographed photo of the weatherman—inscribed *To
my friend*—remained in its frame behind the barber's chair. On
Thursday afternoons, the man in that picture continued to make
his weekly visit to the shop, where the barber's wife would cut
his hair and trim his whiskers, not one word passing between
the lovers that whole time. If other customers were present, the
barber would greet him with his usual unctuous congeniality,
telling jokes and exchanging small talk, as if delighted by the
weatherman's presence. But if the three of them were alone, he
would glare at his adversary through the mirror, his eyes watery
with hate, his fingers wrapped tightly around the handle of a
straight razor, its blade gleaming as he scraped it against the
strop.

IV

One night when the grit seemed to glitter in the moonlight, as
if they were driving through stardust, the weatherman and the
barber's wife wandered far from town. Zigzagging through a
maze of country lanes, bounding over empty pastures, making
one impulsive turn after another, they rushed past any place
they could have later identified on a map. The barber's wife
had been taking more and more risks of late, leaving her seat-
belt unfastened as she smashed the truck through barbed wire
fences or bounced it over gullies. Sometimes, the weatherman
wondered if she hoped to meet the same fate as her son, but on
nights like this, those close calls only seemed to heighten her
sense of purpose and desire.

At length they came to a thin patch of sand that had

once been a beach but now lay landlocked amid dust-bound sailboats and piers that led into nothing. Yanking off their clothes, kicking off their shoes, they walked together into the lakebed, cool silt crunching softly beneath their feet as they traversed a dreamscape of formerly submerged debris—rusted metal drums, ancient tires, the carcass of an all-terrain vehicle that must have fallen through the ice, even a prosthetic arm, reaching out at them from the mud like some lost soul being dragged down to hell. A stagnant pool, smelling of algae and dead fish, was all that remained of the water, and as they made their way toward its distant glimmer, the air began to fill with what looked like snow. Yes, even the weatherman thought so: pure white snow in the middle of summer in the middle of a drought, only it didn't fall to the ground but danced and skimmed across the surface of the earth and rose into the dark. With a great collective shudder, it smothered out the stars, and as the weatherman stared at La Niña through that otherworldly storm, she whispered, *Moths*. Soon, they, too, were covered, the creatures tangling in their hair and caking on their skin like delicate barnacles and massing at their ankles in a deep soft bed. And as they fell to the ground, wrapped in that swarming blanket, the weatherman felt that he and the barber's wife had disappeared, fused with the soil and sky and air and each other into a single elemental thing. It was only much later in an old library book that he came upon a possible entomological explanation. Moths often massed at shallow pools in search of water—a behavior called puddling. Some species were even known to suck tears from the eyes of cattle. The drought, he guessed, had made the poor creatures desperate—attacking the lovers for their sweat.

Even for those of us who lived through those days, such events can seem almost unreal now, like shards of some half-forgotten dream. At the time, however, we had all grown accustomed to strange sights: the black blizzards of wind-whipped topsoil, so dense and dark they turned day into night; the corpses of cattle drowned by the blowing dirt; the gaunt coyotes, placid as poodles as they wandered the streets of town in search of food; the swarms of grasshoppers that emerged from nowhere, devoured entire fields, then vanished again; the abandoned buildings, sandblasted to the bare wood or buried in drifts of dust; the dried-up riverbed behind the barbershop, reeking of rotting fish. But even more perverse and disturbing than the ravages of nature were the actions of our own townspeople. It was not just that crime jumped dramatically during the drought (no surprise, given the high rates of poverty and unemployment), but that we no longer knew what to expect of each other. Anyone seemed capable of anything. A church elder might poison his own family; an old friend might steal one's credit card; the lady next door might burn her home to the ground. No human calamity seemed impossible or even unusual. We became immune to it all—and in so doing we became strangers to one another. When we saw a former coworker on the corner, begging for alms, we averted our eyes and crossed to the other side of the street. When we heard the shrieks of a child at night, we shut our windows and turned on the air conditioner. And when we opened the paper one morning to learn that a local woman, the wife of a barber, had been found dead inside her overturned truck deep in the backcountry, some four miles from the nearest road, we just sighed at one more incomprehensible tragedy, then reached for the sports section.

V

The town had grown so used to the weatherman's presence

that he seemed somehow ubiquitous, like the taste of dust or the howl of the wind. We did not realize we had placed all our hopes in him until the day he failed to show up for work. I handled the situation as well as I could, instructing our news anchor to announce that her colleague was out with a cold and would return soon. Within hours, however, our switchboard was overwhelmed, as rumors swirled through town that the weatherman was gravely ill or dead. At the studio's entrance, a makeshift shrine of flowers, teddy bears, and get-well cards began to rise, and by nightfall, solemn teenagers and housewives were keeping a candlelight vigil.

The following day I received news that a pickup truck had been discovered in the wilderness. Perplexed by reports that there was only one victim, a woman, I had just made up my mind to call the police and request a search for my missing employee, his secret be damned, when I heard a commotion in the newsroom. He was making his way toward my office with a pronounced limp, and when his eyes met mine, it was as if he, not his lover, had died in that truck. I ordered the gawkers back to work, ushered him into my office, and shut the door. He was too distraught to say much, only that she had been killed instantly, that he had stayed with her corpse for more than twenty-four hours until overcome by thirst, and that somehow he had found his way back to his car. His blazer was splattered with blood, his hair filthy and wild. There were cuts on his forehead, and his right wrist, swollen and contorted, appeared to be broken. I asked him if he was ready to go on the air.

Word of his comeback spread quickly. The ratings for that night's six o'clock news broke all local records for the time slot. Through most of the weather segment, however, I thought I had made a mistake in rushing him before the cameras. He was listless and detached, delivering his report in a barely audible murmur, as if reciting it by rote. Halfway through the five-day forecast, he left off in mid-sentence, apparently forgetting his line of thought. He stood there for a moment, his head bowed, a look of confusion on his face. Just as I was about to cut to a commercial, he fell to his knees and began to pray.

VI

On the second-floor lounge of our studio is a row of windows that overlooks the hair salon, and in the months after the accident I would often find the weatherman there, watching. One day, I noticed the barber standing outside the store, staring back. The moment was oddly restrained. It seemed certain that the barber would have known his nemesis was in the truck that night—and equally certain that he would have wanted revenge. Yet both men wore blank, even removed expressions. Made intimates by a shared secret, they seemed to be testing each other, like card players probing one another's faces for a weakness. As the months wore on, I would observe this same peculiar ritual on several other occasions, but to the best of my knowledge they never actually spoke in all that time.

Within weeks of his wife's death, the barber lost most of his business. She had given her customers a sense of beauty and order amid the chaos of drought, and now her husband, caustic and morose, only seemed to remind them of the sadness in their lives. Even his old friends began to shun the shop, as if the place itself was somehow cursed. Most conspicuous among the missing, however, was the man whose photo still hung behind the barber's chair. After the death of La Niña, the weatherman had refused to let anyone, much less the barber, cut his hair. Within a few months, it gnarled into a great unkempt mass— but even that seemed tame when compared with the beard. Long and sinewy and knotted, like some primitive life form, those whiskers seemed to manifest the disorder and despair of the age. With them, the weatherman looked alternately beatific and menacing. Our ratings were never higher.

Increasingly, his broadcasts focused less on the drought itself than on the human dimension of the crisis. He sought housing for the homeless and food for the hungry. He offered prayers for the sick and eulogies for the dead. He praised people who acted compassionately and chastised those who profited from the suffering of others. I was not the only person to notice a new sense of civility creeping into our community, thanks to his efforts. Still, there was no rain.

His spirits darkened steadily as time swept him further from La Niña. Books about meteorology no longer interested him; now he read works of theology, mythology, the history of religion. He told me about the Ihanzu people of East Africa who slit the throat of a specially selected black sheep, its head pointed to the west and tail to the east; the prophets of Baal who cut themselves with knives; the Javanese who thrashed each other with whips until the blood flowed down their backs; the Dieri of southeastern Australia who sprinkled the blood of two medicine men on other members of the group; the Mayans who practiced human sacrifice—all to conjure rain. He began to spend his nights back in the countryside, revisiting old haunts. Sometimes, when he was in the mood for conversation, he would ask me to accompany him on these nocturnal pilgrimages. *We were here,* he would say, pointing to a wind-blown field, or *We were there—under that tree.* And then he would get out of the car and sit down in the dust, his eyes closed, his head tipped back toward the sky. Once, he leaned over and kissed the earth, open-mouthed, the sand clinging to his beard long afterward.

On the morning the clouds burst—the sixth day of the twenty-seventh month—we ran to our windows in stunned silence. The weatherman had promised this the night before, but we could no longer be sure whether his forecasts were based on computer modeling or meditation, and now that the moment was upon us, it seemed so otherworldly as to be frightful. We stood shoulder to shoulder in that second-floor lounge, watching it fall, a sight so magnificent that no one dared speak for fear of being roused out of our collective dream. Then the smell, sweet and electric, began to permeate the room. Our eyes might have been fooled, but our noses could not be. One by one, my coworkers departed, barely saying a word to each other as they dashed out to dance in the rain. At last, only the weatherman and I remained. I watched him as he studied the downpour, a ruminant smile on his face, and then I saw his gaze slip slowly toward the hair salon. The other man was there, in front of that window with the antique barber pole, staring at him through the deluge. They seemed to nod at each other, and then, with a sigh, the weatherman turned to me. *It's time to get a shave,* he said.

Behind the hair salon, the long-dry river was suddenly surging, a flash flood washing away great mounds of fish carcasses and trash. In the streets, people were ripping off their shirts and gargling rainwater and leaping on each other's backs and rolling in puddles and howling and singing songs arm in arm and sobbing with joy and embracing complete strangers. I watched the weatherman make his way through the crowd with steady strides. No one but me saw him slip into the barbershop.

VII

The fields are now full of wheat again, and the children play in lush green lawns. An air of normalcy has returned to our community. It is true that many stores in the center of town remain

closed, but some big chain outlets are going up by the interstate, and everyone seems to agree that this is progress. These
days, we embrace the new. We make a show of ribbon cuttings
and grand openings, of tourism ventures and redevelopment
schemes, of moving on with our lives. Yet beneath all that,
there is an unmistakable feeling of languor and loss, as if we
have squandered our collective sense of purpose. We are less
united, less of a community. Divorce rates are actually higher
than they were during the drought, and many residents who
stayed on through the worst of the crisis have now decided to
leave, complaining of how unfulfilling their lives seem here,
how claustrophobic the place has become.

The barber recently married a chain-smoking divorcée who
works at a telemarketing firm across town, and they seem to
get along well. If you ask him about his first wife, he implores
you, awkwardly and sometimes angrily, to believe how much
he adored her and how good she was to him—but otherwise,
he seems more at ease with himself than in the old days. At
least he no longer has to play second fiddle in his own shop.
Business has slowly returned, but the place looks different. The
weatherman's photo is no longer on the wall, for instance, and
that antique barber pole is also gone. I once asked what had
become of those items. *Tossed them in the river,* he said. Some
patrons laughed, as if he was joking, but the barber's face contained no hint of a smile.

The clientele has also changed dramatically. No longer does
the salon cater to the young, the beautiful, and the ambitious,
those who yearn to keep up with the times, whose imagina-
tions outreach this city. The barber's new customers are old
men. Retirees with nothing to do when the golf courses close
for winter, shopkeepers who went belly-up in the drought, and
senile stragglers from a nursing home that just opened in what

used to be the town's leading department store—they all wait for the barber to unlock his door at 8:00 a.m. When the chair is open, one of them will slide in, out of courtesy if not need, but mostly they just sit around, drinking coffee and flipping through well-worn hunting and girlie magazines, the smell of fresh blood and the feel of firm flesh now but faint memories.

I join these men every weekday on my way to work. Aware that I am a punctual and busy person, they make sure to leave the chair unoccupied at 8:40 each morning. Our ritual is always the same: I glance around the room, greeting those present with a simple recitation of names, and as I sit down and open a golfing magazine, the barber begins to lather my face. Although my station's ratings have slipped back just behind those of the competition, our ad revenues, thanks to the thriving local economy, remain strong. Last Christmas, my employers rewarded me with a generous bonus, which I used for the down payment on a cottage at a local lake. I plan to retire there. For the past four months, I have been dating the widow of a school principal. We have relatively little in common, but she is a pleasant companion, which is more than I could have said about any of my ex-wives. I have been asked to teach a class at the university and to serve on the library board. After all these years, I have a stake in this community. That's one thing all the barber's regulars have in common: the knowledge that we will die in this town. It is, to my surprise, no small bond.

My fellow patrons talk about sports and politics and farming. They talk about the sweet lost days of their youth. They talk about which friends are sick and which ones have died and what's on television. But mostly, like everyone else, they talk about the weatherman. His disappearance has meant that he is more a part of our daily lives than ever, that his story is ongoing, with infinite possible developments and conclusions. A retired police officer has it on good authority that he was assassinated on direct orders of the governor, who feared his entrance into politics. A church elder has observed unusual comings and goings at the house of his neighbor, who, he claims, has a long criminal history and once served time for kidnapping. A professor emeritus insists the weatherman arranged his own disappearance to save himself from being revealed as a charlatan, while the treasurer of a nature society reports that members of his group, hiking in a wilderness area, have made numerous sightings of a figure who flees into the brush whenever they approach. A county water commissioner who travels often with his wife swears he saw a dead ringer for the weatherman, clean-shaven with bleached-blond hair, sipping rioja at a café in Barcelona.

Far from being tormented by guilt, a desire to confess, the barber seems strangely comforted by these discussions. He says nothing, but sometimes as he leans over me, my face veiled in the spearmint warmth of his breath, I see—or perhaps I only imagine—a faint smile pass across his lips. He must be tempted to speak, to throw off tantalizing clues, to leave us wondering what he knows. He maintains his silence, however, because that silence is his revenge on this town. Once again he has what everyone covets: this time he is not about to give it away. And perhaps, like me, he understands that in telling the story he would lose his place in it. His secret intact, he can believe that he was a central figure rather than a bit player, that the weatherman walked into the salon that day to answer to him.

In the end, I cannot say if the weatherman was deluded or sane, self-destructive or God-inspired. All I know is that he thought he could bring rain. And for that, I will always envy him. Sometimes, as I sit beneath the barber, the manuscript containing these words folded neatly into the breast pocket of my suit, I wonder what it would be like to believe you can put things right in the world. Sometimes, I swear I will take these pages to the police. But mostly I just close my eyes, let the sound of the old men's chatter wash over me, and concentrate on the push of the razor against my neck, each whisker stretching taut then sliding free.

BEACHCOMBERS IN
DOGGERLAND

Six years ago on this very day at this very beach, a young man rose with the dawn, crawled from his tent, stripped naked, and pulled on his wetsuit. He did not attempt to wake his friends, recent class of 2000 high school graduates from Michigan who, to mark their final days together before heading off to college, had piled into a couple of cars and driven nineteen sleepless hours to this state park on Florida's Treasure Coast. A week later, the boy's father would read a newspaper interview with one of those young people, a girl who had never camped before and kept startling awake to the slightest sound. According to the report, she heard the young man curse under his breath as he tripped over a trash bag full of empty beer cans. Peeking out through the mesh of her doorway, she watched him gather his surfboard and stroll off with long, lanky strides, his impressive muddle of curly brown hair bouncing ostentatiously as he made his way toward the beach. Because the campground overlooked the water, she could see him wade in, climb belly down onto the board, and paddle out into the waves. Then, as the girl would explain in that interview, she lost sight of him, his silhouette disappearing into the first fierce burst of sunrise.

Although the father has known this young woman since she starred with his son in an eighth-grade production of *The Lion King* (the boy as a pimply Mufasa, the girl as Rafiki, badly off-key in "Circle of Life"), they've only spoken a couple of times since the incident. She seemed scared of him, as if he somehow blamed her for his son's disappearance—no corpse, no clues, even the surfboard gone without a trace. And perhaps he does blame her, not just for surviving, not just for telling her story to reporters before she recounted it in less detail to him, not just for having no answers, but for moving on while his life stands still. The girl who played Rafiki is in law school now, while he and his wife are back on this same beach with their fifteen-year-old daughter. Unlike the sweltering day when the boy vanished, this morning is chilly, a dense fog giving the whole coastline the dreamlike appearance of a faded photograph. Nothing has substance except the iodine smell of the sea, so potent it seems to dull all his other senses, lulling him into a waking dream. One moment, his wife is standing right next to him on the beach. The next, without an instant appearing to pass, she's wading into the water, fully clothed.

"I see something," she says.

"Where?" her husband asks.

"Out there," she replies, pointing into the gray haze of the horizon.

The man stares into the mist but can't make out anything besides slow-rolling waves, and then it occurs to him that his wife doesn't see anything either. He turns to his daughter, who sits on a dune that leads down to the beach, yanking handfuls of seagrass from the sand. She glances back, bulky headphones clamped tight over close-cropped hair, iPod blasting some punk band so loud he can hear the tinny throb ten yards away. Then she rises and begins to trudge toward him in the black leather jacket and beat-up combat boots she wears almost everywhere. Nine years the missing boy's junior, she's as inward as he was extroverted, as apprehensive as he was carefree, as unsure of herself as he was brash. As she approaches, the man feels a sudden desire to reach out and embrace her, but she just gives him an angry glare and marches past down the beach.

"Good luck," she says over her shoulder. "This year, he's sure to show up."

"Don't be nasty," he says, but she just keeps walking.

His wife is now knee-deep in the surf, her jeans and cardigan losing their color as she fades into the fog. In this amorphous state, she seems somehow smaller and more fragile, and it occurs to him that perhaps what he sees is no optical illusion. Although she's good at keeping up appearances, his wife has always been restless, painfully unsure about her place in the world. While he comes from a close-knit family, she's the only child of an unhappy marriage. Her father left when she was a toddler—one final abandonment for her mother who was raised in a series of foster homes after her parents had died in the concentration camps during World War II, a lonely upbringing that left the woman with little aptitude for, or interest in, raising a child. As a result, the man's wife was denied something that most children get, even in a rudimentary fashion, something that makes the world seem solid, which is love.

He wants to run to her now, take her by the hand and lead her back to shore, but he's always been afraid of water, a phobia that goes back to swimming lessons at the YMCA on the corner of West Maple and Hudson Street in Kalamazoo, where, at age six, he would wet his swim trunks while waiting in line for the instructor, a huge, gruff man with a hairy back, to throw him into the pool. This terror has only intensified since his son's disappearance, especially today when the water seems to be pressing in on him from the air as well as the sea. He takes a couple of steps toward his wife then stops, paralyzed by the sight of the surf licking at the sand. Short of breath, he watches his spouse dissolve into a curtain of vapor that gives him the sensation of teetering over a void, suddenly unable to shake the idea that this woman who works at the circulation desk of the public library and serves as secretary of the local League of Women Voters, this woman who sleeps next to him every night and starts the coffee every morning and drives their child to school, orthodontist appointments, and visits to the therapist, this same woman who was just standing on solid earth, is somehow an apparition. Present and absent, there and not—just like the melody he now hears emerging from the mist, a wordless tune, beautiful and haunting, which his wife sometimes hums when she's anxious or excited or deep in thought, especially when she assumes he's not listening.

Kicking off his sandals, he wills himself into the water, but the cold surf staggers him like a live wire, jolting his whole body and causing him to leap back. Wheeling around, he sees that his daughter, too, is fading away. He calls her name, but she doesn't respond, just stomps off through the mist as if she's trying to bully it into lifting. In those first few months after the disappearance, his wife had doted on the girl, not even letting her out of her sight after bedtime, when she'd sit in her room for hours, watching her sleep while humming the same mournful tune he's hearing now. But over the years, he has sensed the woman slowly pushing their surviving child away. It's not anything she has said out loud, just a coolness that has grown into a kind of unstated antipathy that the girl can't help but to feel—and to return. On public TV not long ago, he saw a documentary about Doggerland, the name for some underwater terrain that once connected England and Northern Europe before rising ocean levels submerged it almost eight millennia ago. And now, as he watches his daughter vanish in one direction and his wife in another, he thinks whatever it was which once held his family together has long since gone the way of that doomed landmass, swallowed by the sea.

At his feet, a sand-colored crab skitters around on hairy legs, moving sideways, then backward, before suddenly shooting away, as if in panic. The man can barely make out his wife, a smudge in the mist, the waves by now above her waist.

"Can you see what it is?" he shouts.

"No, but I feel it."

Her voice sounds far away. "Feel what?"

"It's here. I can almost touch it," he hears her say. Then there's silence. Then the song. The sea air feels suffocating. Why do they keep making these annual beachcombing pilgrimages? What do they hope to find? Most of the stuff they bring home, after all, is just junk—soda bottles, cigarette lighters, polystyrene food containers, running shoes, tennis balls, fishing nets, buoys, wooden pallets, and oil drums. But other objects are mystifying. Once, they found a plastic bride-and-groom figurine from a wedding cake, paint scoured off by the ocean, facial features eroded away. Judging by the hair and clothing styles of those figurines, the object could have been fifty or sixty years old. But where had it come from? How long had it been floating around? And what had become of the real bridal couple, the flesh-and-blood one?

He can no longer see his wife. All that remains of her is the song, which seems to rise from the fog itself, everywhere, yet evanescent. In the early years of their marriage, he used to ask her about this haunting melody, which sometimes reminds him of a lullaby, sometimes of a dirge, but she would just shrug. There are so many things she keeps to herself, so many things he doesn't understand. It was not normally like her, for example, to wade into the water with all her clothes on. If anything, his wife of twenty-three years has been rational and fastidious to a fault. But ever since their beachcombing began, she's become increasingly impulsive. Last year, the two of them were strolling the shoreline on a windy, overcast afternoon when, without a word, his wife turned, splashed into the crashing waves, and returned a few minutes later, soaked to skin, something cradled in her arms like an infant. Just more driftwood, the man had initially assumed, but as she came closer he saw that despite its sea-weathered state, the thing was man-made, a lathed cylinder about three feet long with spherical shapes on each end, like an old-fashioned dumbbell. And as his wife reached shore, shivering and breathless, he could make out something even more unusual. Although its colors were badly faded, the piece of wood had once been painted white with twisting blue, red, and white stripes. The next day, while his wife and daughter were at the grocery store, he took the arti-fact to a local antiques dealer who confirmed what the man already suspected. The relic, he said, was a wooden barbershop pole, perhaps one hundred years old.

"But how is that possible?"

The dealer shrugged.

"It happens," he said. "Every so often, the ocean coughs up some cargo from the deep that defies rational explanation. I don't get too shocked about it anymore."

People had come into his shop with all manner of beach-combing oddities, he added, including a tortoiseshell hair comb from the 1700s, a fully intact rolltop desk, circa 1910, and a barnacle-encrusted piece of the Space Shuttle Challenger. And just last year, he said, the shipwrecked hull of a nineteenth-century vessel had suddenly appeared on a beach in northern Florida. The thing was huge—forty-eight feet long and twelve feet wide, with the ribs of its frame almost completely intact. But what was weirdest of all is that it had seemingly come out of nowhere. There was nothing special about the water currents on the day it washed in, nothing unusual about the weather.

"Ever heard of the littoral zone?" the antiques dealer asked.

"Something to do with the shoreline, right?"

"Yes, sir. It's the part that's above ocean level at low tide and underwater when the tide is high. Not quite land, not quite sea. And sometimes I can't help but think of it as an in-between place for past and present as well. Anything is possible there."

And now, shouting his wife's name, he forces himself into this same littoral zone, unsure whether his convulsions are from cold or fear, certain only he needs to reach her before something terrible happens, something he should have seen coming. For the past couple of years, she's become obsessed with omens and revelations—crazy talk, dangerous talk, the kind of talk people use before they do something desperate. That's why he swore not to reveal what the antiques dealer said about that barbershop pole, which he'd originally planned to throw back into the sea but couldn't part with when the time came. Instead, he hid it away—a secret known only to his daughter, who happened upon him in the hotel parking lot just as he was stashing that thing in the wheel well of the car trunk. He begged her not to say anything, the only time he's ever asked the young woman to lie to her mother, then waited until the night they got back to Kalamazoo before telling his wife that he must have left the pole back at their room in Florida. There was a scene and then there was a silence, one that has settled over the house ever since, as thick and forbidding as the fog into which she has now vanished.

He stops, calf-deep in the waves, gasping for air and trying to determine the direction of the song, but all he can tell is that it's moving out to sea. She's been drifting away from him for years, though sometimes he thinks it's his own doing, like when he brought the barber pole back to the house, moving it from hiding place to hiding place, never sure whether he wanted to protect her from it or keep it to himself. Then he hit on an idea, irrational but irresistible, the impulse for which he still doesn't completely understand. Using spare scraps of plywood, he built a rectangular box, lined it with velour and fitted it with a lid, which he screwed shut after placing the pole inside. One Saturday, when he knew his wife and daughter would be gone, he rolled back the carpet in the master bedroom, pulled up some floorboards and placed the wooden box between a couple of joists. Now he and his wife sleep over it every night. Occasionally, unable to calm his mind in the late hours, he feels as if there's a time bomb beneath him. But on most nights, he finds it strangely comforting to know the box is there, his own song, his own private littoral zone between past and present, his own secret from his wife. He wants to put his child to rest. Why did it take him so long to understand that the thing he'd buried beneath their floor was a coffin?

For his wife, the search for their son will never be satisfied. He's sure of that now, shivering in the surf as that faint melody fades in and out. The air is so thick it seems to break up time the way it does space, every second suddenly discrete, unconnected to the one before it. A young man on a run emerges from the mist two feet in front of him, staring straight ahead as if unaware of his presence, then vanishes mid-stride. He tries to picture how his boy ran, how he moved. No image comes to mind. He listens for the sound of footfalls. None reach him. He calls his wife again. Nothing. He pictures her walking slowly, steadily, as the waves crash over her head, as the sea consumes her. Is she capable of such a thing? He listens for the song but hears only the draw and push of his own breath as he splashes forward, tripping into the surf, soaking his clothes, feeling the unbearable weight of the sea on his skin. A plastic bottle floats past, its label in some language he doesn't recognize. He thinks of the traces of Doggerland that keep showing up in fishing nets—a human jawbone, part of a human skull, animal bones carved by human hands with mysterious zigzagging lines, flint tools, spear points, a whole world that still exists on the ocean floor. Suddenly, he can almost feel the ocean retreating in front of him, siphoning into some giant drain at the center of the world to reveal everything that's ever been lost: Spanish treasure ships, their holds packed with silver and gold; transatlantic sea liners and freighters and fishing trawlers and U-boats and luxury yachts with cases of expensive champagne still cooling in the refrigerator; bottles stuffed with soggy notes that never reached the eyes of strangers; wedding rings, bronze cannons, can tabs, antique brass compasses, shipping containers full of Barbie dolls and cell phones and vacuum cleaners and car tires and sex toys and packages of heroin, endless items blown overboard and thrown overboard; mafiosos limping around with cements blocks on their feet and drunkards sleeping it off on beds of seaweed; pirates and explorers and Vikings and long-distance swimmers and dirigible pilots and kite surfers and clumsy cruise ship passengers, whole crowds sloshing around in the muck. And out there, still out of sight amid this vast jungle of wreckage, stands his son.

Stumbling forward, the man screams, "Where are you?"

"Where the hell are you?" he yells again.

He waits for a shout or a song from the thickening fog but hears only waves rolling under and under and under and back under, always disappearing into the sea.

THE MAN WHO SLEPT
WITH EUDORA WELTY

The encounter I am about to describe took place in October or November of 1990, late at night, during an Amtrak trip from Chicago to Ann Arbor. On that route in those days, it was not uncommon for trains to make unexplained stops miles from the nearest town, then sit for hours. For the most part, as I recall, passengers took such delays in stride, sleeping or killing time talking to strangers or, in my case, trying to read. On this night, we were stuck on a bridge over some small river, a fact that I remember because of the view out my window—the ruin of another bridge, concrete and unrailed, which no longer spanned the ravine. It stuck out there, high on its single foot, like a table in the water. Every so often I would glance out at its moonlit silhouette, then return to my book. On one of these occasions, however, I must've nodded off to sleep for a minute or two, because I suddenly looked up to discover that an old man was now sprawled in the seat facing mine, having somehow managed to slide in without me noticing.

He must have been in his late seventies, maybe early eighties. His eyes were gray and unlit and dingy, as if peering out at me through soiled windows of an abandoned old house, though I remember little else about his face. My impression is that he was, or had once been, handsome. His suit—red plaid, as I recall—was wrinkled and years out of fashion, but his necktie was neatly knotted. In each hand he clutched a miniature Dewar's bottle, the right one still capped, the left one suspended below his lips in a state of permanent readiness, the way a child holds a half-licked lollipop. Every minute or so, he'd take a precise birdlike sip. Although he smelled of alcohol and unchanged clothes and microwaved pizza from the dining car, he held himself with an air of swagger and ironic disdain. He kept staring at the back cover of my book and chuckling to himself.

"Is that old what's-her-name?" he finally said in a sleepy southern drawl. "The legendary writer lady?"

I flipped the book over and glanced at the black-and-white jacket photo—an elderly woman with mousy white hair, cat-eye glasses, buck teeth, big ears, and no chin.

"Eudora Welty?" I asked.

"Eudora, yes!" he said, laughing to himself again. "Ah, Eudora, Eudora, Eudora."

He took a sip and closed his eyes, as if lost in some happy thought. Our conversation, it seemed, had ended as abruptly and oddly as it began, so I opened *Delta Wedding* and tried to find my place. At the University of Michigan, where I was then pursuing an MFA in creative writing, my teachers and colleagues all seemed infatuated with Welty, whom they invariably referred to by her first name, as if she was somebody's great aunt. Tired of feeling left out, and too embarrassed to confess my total ignorance of her work, I had quietly vowed to give myself a crash course, which I thought of as Welty 101. It was not going well. I'd begun that night with her first full novel, the plot of which, coincidentally, opened on a train. But her long description of the fictional world going past outside the window had not seemed nearly as interesting as the real world outside my own. I kept opening the book, reading a sentence or two, then putting it down, unable to maintain focus. The stranger's presence only made matters worse.

Looking up, I saw him eyeing me again with a drowsy sneer.

"Quite a woman," he said.

"You've read her books?"

"No sir, never. But on occasion she used to recite a few pages to me."

"You knew her?"

"Oh, hell yes," he said. "I knew Eudora. I definitely knew Eudora."

His laugh was languorous and creaky, a weathered door swinging open into a dark hallway. It felt like an invitation, and though I knew I shouldn't take him up on it, I found myself unable to resist. Soon he was telling me about his days as a travelling salesman, hawking sewing machines across Mississippi. He'd met Welty, or so he claimed, in 1936, when she was a photographer for the Works Progress Administration.

"This was before she became your legendary writer lady," he said. "The government was paying her to go around taking pictures of people. Can you imagine? Well, she was out in Oktibbeha County to get a shot of some big fat blind woman who made useless whatnots on a loom. That night, your author and me, we wound up two doors down from each other at the same hotel. Only it turned out we didn't need both of them beds."

He leaned back and laughed, then took a sip.

"Lordy, lordy, sweet Eudorie," he sighed.

Although I was unfamiliar with the actual circumstances of Welty's life, I felt certain that the whole lurid tale must be a fabrication. And yet this stranger seemed to know so much about the woman—details he couldn't have made up. Not only did he recount the Tudor-style house where she lived with her widowed mother in Jackson, for instance, but he also described the old water oak in the front yard and the magenta-blossomed camellias beneath her bedroom window.

"In that line of work," he continued, "I drove around so much I sometimes forgot what town I was in and which town I was bound for. But whenever I happened into Jackson, I would dial up old Eudora. 'The famous *he*'—that's what she called me, who knows why. 'Well, well, what's the famous *he* doing in town?' And I'd say, 'I come from afar, sweetheart, to see you.' And more often than not, she'd make up some excuse to her mama and meet me at my car near her house. Sometimes we'd go out to the country on this little gravel road until we found a nice private place to park. Other times, we'd just head to the motor court out there on Route 18. Such a little slight thing, your author. But get a glass or two of Memphis whisky in her and hoo-boy!"

In lazy cadence but urgent detail, the stranger then launched into a long description of their supposed exploits, both in bed and in the back seat of his DeSoto. He could tell this litany embarrassed me, and I could tell my embarrassment gave him pleasure. I sat there silently, feeling guilty and complicit and trapped. A woman sitting across the aisle shot him an outraged glance, then aimed an even more accusing one at me, while someone a few rows back shushed us angrily. But the stranger only let out another raspy laugh, gave me a conspiratorial grin, and resumed his tale. I tried to remember whether Welty was still alive and wished she wasn't, as if that fact could have somehow spared her from this indignity, but then I remembered a friend telling me he'd just heard an interview with her on public radio. And suddenly, although I'd never before felt the slightest emotional attachment to this famous figure, I began to think my presence in that conversation constituted a personal betrayal of her in some way.

Without attempting to offer an excuse, I grabbed the novel and got to my feet. The man said nothing, just took a draw of scotch and flashed a self-satisfied smile as I walked away. Finding a seat in the dining car, I opened *Delta Wedding* and tried to read but once again found it impossible to concentrate. Conductors kept coming and going, conversing loudly on their walkie-talkies with unseen colleagues whose staticky voices sounded thousands of miles away. Every now and then, one of these uniformed men would say, "Folks, we'll have this mechanical problem taken care of soon," a claim seemingly belied by the frantic metal-on-metal knocking sounds outside, as if somebody were beating a wrench against the engine in a desperate effort to make it start. A line formed at the concession stand, and at the rear of it I thought I spotted the stranger. But on second glance, I concluded the man bore no resemblance to my recent acquaintance, and then it occurred to me that I lacked a clear picture of him in my mind. Finally, I decided to return to my seat, resolving that I wouldn't allow him to humiliate me like that again. When I got there, however, he was gone. He never came back. The train surged forward, and the anxious mood I'd been in since meeting him started to lift. I glanced down at *Delta Wedding* and noticed a beautiful passage: *The land was perfectly flat and level but it shimmered like the wing of a lighted dragonfly. It seemed strummed, as though it were an instrument and something had touched it.* By the time we arrived in Ann Arbor, I was halfway through the book. Exiting the train, I spotted two miniature bottles on the floor, both empty. For a second, I considered keeping them as souvenirs, then thought the better of it and flipped them in the trash.

When I got up the next morning, the previous night's encounter seemed strangely distant and indistinct, as if I had been the one drinking too much scotch. I'd been looking forward to regaling my graduate-school friends, Bill and Mike and Cammie and Beth, with an ironic account of the incident during one of our regular drunken meetings at the Colonial Lanes bowling alley. But suddenly I began to have second thoughts. Back on the train I'd been ashamed of listening to the man's stories, but now I felt angry with myself for not paying enough attention. Had he told me his name? How did he wind up sitting across from me? Where did he board that train and what was his destination? And above all, was it possible that the things he'd said were true? If the stranger had played a trick on me, I wasn't sure I wanted anyone else to know about it. And if he was who he claimed to be, I was determined to track down his identity on my own.

I began at the University of Michigan library that very day, poring through books and articles about the author, who, I quickly learned, was unmarried and childless, having resided for all but a few short periods in the home of her parents. Although Welty was notoriously silent about her private life, most biographers concluded, or at least strongly implied, that she'd never had any sexual relationships. Once, in her early thirties, she supposedly confided to fellow writer Katherine Anne Porter that she was still a virgin, to which the acerbic Porter was said to reply, "Yes, dear, and you always will be." This exchange seems to have taken place around 1941—five years *after* the man on the train claimed to have begun sleeping with Welty. The facts, it seemed, sharply contradicted his version of events. Yes, but how had he known so much about her? Hadn't he mentioned the name of her street? Didn't he, in fact, tell me the exact number of her house? Could my memory already be playing tricks on me, or did I hear him say "1119

Pinehurst," the address I'd just come across on page twenty-two of one of her biographies?

I turned to Welty's fiction, hoping I might find him there. After finishing *Delta Wedding*, I spent the next few days flipping back and forth through the 622 pages of the *Collected Stories*. Almost everything in the book seemed at odds with her image as a cloistered innocent. Her tales, I discovered, were wild with sexual longing and illicit encounters—one taking place on a dirty mattress in an abandoned house, another on a spot of high ground above a cemetery flooded by the Mississippi, a third near the ruin of an old bridge that looked "like a table in the water." They were also full of restless drifters and travelling salesmen, one of whom, like the man on that train, even trafficked in sewing machines. In his spare time, this fictional figure liked to open his maroon-colored bathrobe and expose himself to strangers—which, the more I thought about it, was not unlike what the mysterious passenger had done to me that night.

But it was in another tale about a travelling salesman where I finally thought I caught a glimpse of my seatmate. His name was Tom Harris, the rootless protagonist of "The Hitch-Hikers," one of Welty's better-known pieces of short fiction. Harris drifts through the South selling office supplies, an existence void of time, place, and meaning, his world consisting only of the next town, the next round of drinks with strangers, the next hotel, the next woman. "Just old Harris passin' through"—that's how one man refers to him in a village where the salesman ends up spending the night. Although he goes to parties and carouses with the townspeople, he's the eternal exile, a bystander in incidents and lives to which he has no real connection. The only character capable of seeing him as a kindred soul is a young woman who knew Harris a few years earlier when he was still full of youthful enthusiasm. She recalls him at a summer dance, joyfully playing piano while exclaiming, "Now this is how it really is!" But Harris claims not to remember the incident. "Maybe," he says, "you've got the wrong man."

Was the young woman in that story—spurned by the salesman after she declares her love for him—Welty herself? And was that stranger on the train an elderly Tom Harris? Or did I, too, have the wrong man? I've read "The Hitch-Hikers" dozens of times over the past thirty years, and I'm less sure than ever. Reality and fiction, it seems, have only become more and more muddled in my mind. Earlier in this account, for example, I wrote that the man on the train claimed Welty always called him "the famous *he*." And to the best of my recollection, that's true. But it's also true that one of the female characters in "The Hitch-Hikers" uses that exact phrase to describe Tom Harris. Did I somehow absorb this snippet of fictional dialogue into my memories of the incident? Did Welty put those words, which she'd once whispered to her own lover, on the lips of a proxy character? Or was the actual situation even more complicated? On certain nights, as I lie in bed listening to the sound of my ceiling fan, I like to entertain the idea that my fellow passenger was a man of letters—perhaps even a professor of English, as I myself have become in my later years. In my imagination, he's wandering the aisle of the Amtrak when he notices a young man reading a book by a familiar author. On a sudden impulse, perhaps inspired by scotch, he decides to play a trick on the stranger. Sitting down across from him, he assumes the role of one of Welty's characters, even sprinkling in a few direct quotes from her stories for the sake of a laugh. Perhaps he hopes the reader will get this literary prank, maybe even play along. But when the man turns out to be an ignorant philistine, he decides to turn the joke around, make a fool of his new acquaintance by transforming a highbrow hoax into a piece of pornography. Little does he know that the man will spend the rest of his life searching for the instigator of this impromptu fraud. Little does he know that years from now, when that same man, now a writer himself, finally tries to get the encounter down in words, he will be unable to determine whether he's the author of the old man's story or the other way around.

There's a scene from "The Hitch-Hikers" in which Tom Harris accompanies some of the locals on a drunken ramble far out into the countryside just so they can stand on a bridge and scream into the rainy night. Some of them hear a distant echo, while others can't make out any sound at all. "There's nothing anywhere," one of them says—and in the three decades since I first read that story, I've often felt the same way. Although I've searched for the stranger in almost everything Eudora Welty ever wrote—her novels and her memoir and her books about the alchemy of storytelling—he remains like that echo, so faint as to seem almost imperceptible. Over the course of those years, in fact, a curious reversal has taken place. While the man on the train has transmogrified from a flesh-and-blood human being to a phantom of the mind, the fictional Tom Harris has become ever more real, so much so that at this exact moment I have a precise image of his face—the way he smiles without looking the other person in the eye, for instance, or the way his cheek twitches when something surprises or amuses him. In my sixties, I've also come to know his exhaustion of the soul, that sleep-deprived sense of being too drained by the world "to move out of this lying still clothed on the bed, even into comfort or despair."

Welty once wrote that the primary challenge of an author is "to imagine yourself inside another person," a metamorphosis she described as "making the jump." And over the years, I've gone from admiring her ability to inhabit the lives of fictional characters to feeling that the border between those lives and my own is increasingly porous, with all sorts of phenomena making the jump. Recently, for example, I was reading her story "June Recital" when I came upon a passage about "a funny, ugly doll" called a Billiken—a good luck charm, shaped like a grinning Buddha with huge, pointed ears, that serves as the unlikely mascot of St. Louis University, the college that my eighteen-year-old son had, on that very day, decided to attend. A couple of months earlier, while I was finishing a short story about a barber-shop pole that suddenly appears after someone's death, I happened to open my tattered copy of *Collected Works* to page 102, a passage from "Flowers for Marjorie" in which a man who, after killing his pregnant girlfriend and rushing into the street, spots "a thin gray cat watching in front of a barber's pole." And just now, while once again rereading "The Hitch-Hikers," I became aware of something I had never consciously noticed before: that one of the characters sings "The One Rose That's Left in My Heart," the same Jimmie Rodgers tune I'd selected, seemingly at random, for a different story about a character who loves old-time country music.

Mere coincidences, perhaps, but whenever they happen, I feel both the shudder of recognition and the joy of being recognized, as if someone else is observing my life from the other side of the page. Now on the verge of old age, I've known many kinds of intimacy—the complex pleasures of marriage, the endless anxieties and satisfactions of raising children, the bittersweet goodbyes with dying loved ones, and the enduring consolations of long-lasting friendships (including those with my graduate school colleagues from all those years ago in Ann Arbor). But these days, few human beings feel closer to my heart than the woman who once declared that her "continuing passion" as a writer was "to part a curtain, that invisible shadow that falls between people, the veil of indifference to each other's presence, each other's wonder, each other's human plight."

Ah, Eudora, Eudora, Eudora. In the end, I can't tell whether the tale I've just told about you is true or false, autobiography or fiction. Nor am I sure why I bothered to write it down. All I can say for certain is that you've made the jump into me and perhaps I've made the jump into you, "a shared act of the imagination" between writer and reader, as you once put it. And what you've taught me, sweet Eudora, is that this shared act is perhaps as close a relationship as two people can have. So come, my love. Wrap your arms around me as I sit at the piano. Kiss me on the neck while I play this song.

Now this is how it is, Eudora. This is how it really is!

POSTCARD FROM A FUNERAL, CUMBERLAND, MARYLAND, OCTOBER 10, 1975

Part One: 1993

She will find it in an abandoned farmhouse in Central Illinois—windows shattered, roof cratered, clapboard stripped bare by sun and wind, doorframe empty except for shadows—just the sort of place she and Crazyboy are always seeking out, summer nights spent wandering country roads for some new ruin to call their own.

She will find it inside a desk, the rolltop door locked shut for who knows how many years before Meg and Crazyboy happened upon it just now in a first-floor bedroom carpeted with fallen plaster and pigeon shit. Crazyboy likes to say that he has no faith in human beings, so why should he believe in ghosts, but sometimes Meg can't help wondering about the people who lived in these old places. It's not that she imagines phantom farmwives amid the shadows, watching silently while she and Crazyboy smash the windows or spray-paint obscenities on the walls or spread out their blanket and fuck on the floor. It's just that every now and then fragments of their lives seem to flash through her mind, startling yet elusive, like the

bats that burst past at entranceways to these crumbling structures, stopping her breath before disappearing into the night.

They're like lucid dreams, these moments, as if she's glimpsing scenes through a stranger's eyes—a bee sting at the nape of a little boy's neck, his bare shoulders rising and falling, the sound of his breath; a mason jar of preserved peaches smashing onto a basement floor, green glass scattering, syrup oozing into cracks in the dirty concrete; the muscular shoulders of a sleeping man, his skin tinted orange by the dim light of a kerosene lamp; the shapeless night through a screen window, fireflies sparking and fading, cicadas clamoring and quieting, an infant starting to cry from a few feet away in the darkened room. And now it's happening again: the fingers of a woman's hand opening to reveal a tiny key resting on the palm. As always happens in these hallucinations, the face is just out of sight, but Meg suddenly wonders if that hand might somehow be her own. The feel of cool metal on the fingertips, the key turning in the latch of a rolltop desk, the tiny latch tumbling. Maybe they should get out of this house, leave the desk alone, Meg thinks, seized by the idea that it contains something secret, something she yearns to see, something she's not supposed to find. But just then, Crazyboy steps into the beam of her flashlight, dragging his fraying canvas duffel bag across the floor and signaling for her to back away.

I went across the river and I lay down to sleep
I went across the river and I lay down to sleep

He loves to sing old-time country songs as they ransack these places. There's a smirk on his face as he kneels down to open the duffel bag, but his voice is sweet and slow and clear without a hint of irony or anger.

I went across the river and I lay down to sleep
When I woke up I had shackles on my feet

He always brings that duffel bag with him on their adventures. Inside is a crowbar, a couple of joints, a fifth of Jim Beam, a few cans of spray paint, a wool blanket, a box of condoms, a Polaroid camera, and an axe, the wooden handle of which he's tightening his fingers around now.

It takes a worried man to sing a worried song
It takes a worried man to sing a worried song

Tall and blond, Crazyboy is beautiful. That's not just Meg's opinion; she can tell that everybody thinks so, even the preppy girls at Joliet Central who laugh at his red cowboy boots and his Hank Williams Sr. tattoo, even her mom, who has forbidden Meg from seeing him because he got suspended for putting that boy who made fun of him in the hospital, even her so-called stepmother, who is twenty-nine and buys weed from Crazyboy and wears babydoll dresses when she knows he's coming over and lies to Meg's mom about whether he's still hanging around on the two nights per week Meg has to stay at her dad's place. And her dad, her full-of-himself father, who's normally so busy running his Acura dealership and playing golf and hanging out at that new riverboat casino and trying to keep up with his child bride that he barely notices anything going on with Meg—even he makes cracks about how his brainy, big-hipped daughter could wind up with such a handsome guy.

It takes a worried man to sing a worried song
I'm worried now but I won't be worried long

Crazyboy levels the axe over the desk, one hand near the butt end of the handle, the other way up by the blade. If her mother saw him now, it would confirm all her beliefs—that Crazyboy is sure to ruin Meg's future, just like her ex-husband, whom she married straight out of high school, destroyed her own; that all men are psychopaths; and that this fact justifies drinking dry martinis while still in your waitress uniform after getting home from a breakfast shift at the Ham 'N' Egger. But Meg knows a secret about Crazyboy—the key to his charisma, which only she understands. His left eye is filled with menace, the right one with tenderness. She could never explain how she knows this or why it makes him beautiful, so she doesn't say anything about it, not even to him, but she's sure it's true. What she's not sure of is which eye to trust. Sometimes, as she holds him tight on the filthy floor of one of these old houses, she remembers an image she saw on TV when Hurricane Andrew hit last year—a drenched newswoman clinging to a light pole to keep from getting carried away by the wind, only Meg can never quite decide whether Crazyboy is the pillar or the storm.

Twenty-nine links of chain around my leg
There was twenty-nine links of chain around my leg

With his skinny arms, he brings the axe high above his head, his back arched. Suddenly, he seems comical, like something out of Looney Tunes—Wile E. Coyote stepping into the middle of the road, axe raised, right before getting flattened by that bus. Destined to lose—maybe this is how other people see him, Meg thinks, picturing the forlorn coyote pancaked to the pavement as the Roadrunner, watching him from the back window of the bus, gives a final meep-meep and pulls down a shade emblazoned with "The End." Meg feels something rising up, something she can't suppress, which starts as a laugh but comes out as a half-stifled scream. At the top of his swing, just before letting the axe crash down, Crazyboy glances back at her, his left eye gleaming.

Twenty-nine links of chain around my leg
And upon each link there's an initial of my name

The blade misses the slats and lodges in the top of the desk with a dull crackle. Crazyboy wrenches it from the wood with a vicious tug, just like that time he got mad in the library parking lot and grabbed Meg's arm and yanked her out of the car, her right shoulder sore for weeks afterward. She keeps telling herself that he's never actually hit her—but once, when he saw her talking to another boy at school, he pushed her up against the lockers and smacked his open hand against the metal an inch from her ear. The noise seemed to ring up and down that hallway for a very long time.

Well, the train arrived, it's sixteen coaches long
The train arrived, sixteen coaches long

Now he's raising that axe again, and now he's smashing it into the desk over and over and over, the blade a glimmering blur in the beam of Meg's flashlight, shards of wood spinning into the dark like Chinese firecrackers. She thinks of the kids at school, the ones who gave him his nickname, the ones who stood there snickering in the hallway that day. It must amuse them to no end that a straight-A student, a girl with a future, has wound up with someone like him. But Meg sees sides of Crazyboy that they'll never see. Like how he knows all the constellations, pointing them out one night through a hole in the roof after they made love on the rickety landing of a front-hall staircase, Draco the Dragon and Boötes the Herdsman and Ophiuchus the Serpent Wrestler locked in an eternal battle with a giant snake. ("Like me and my stepdad," he said. "He'll keep beating the shit out of me, and I'll keep coming right back at him.") Or how he has all these 78 rpm records by old-time musicians, Jimmie Rodgers yodeling "The One Rose That's Left in my Heart" and the Carter Family wailing "East Virginia Blues No. 1" and Charlie Poole growling "Take a Drink," a collection that used to belong to his dad, who died of an overdose when Crazyboy was six. Or how he handles those old discs as if they were sacred objects. Or how he turns out all the lights in his basement and plays them for her, singing along to the scratchy recordings in a little-boy whisper.

The train arrived, sixteen coaches long
The woman I love, she's on that train and gone

There's a big jagged hole in the rolltop now, but he keeps flailing away. Through the spray of splinters and swirl of dust, Meg tries to make out what's inside. Why are she and Crazyboy always breaking into things? What are they looking for? Meg remembers a story he told her one night in the darkness of his basement about these two musicians, A. P. Carter and Lesley Riddle, who drove around the South in the 1930s collecting songs. Carter would write down the lyrics and Riddle would memorize the melodies. ("Dude had such a good ear they called him 'the Human Tape Recorder,'" Crazyboy said.) It made her happy to think that those two men had some kind of purpose to their wandering, saving music from oblivion. All she and Crazyboy have ever managed to save are the trophies from their adventures that he stores inside his locker at school. They've saved a faded color photo of three sad-looking men with pompadours, a TV Guide from 1977 with Donnie and Marie Osmond on the cover, and some old coins covered with indecipherable writing and images of rulers in crowns and turbans. But what they're really trying to save, Meg has come to believe, is themselves. On one of their excursions, they found an antique metal penny bank shaped like some naked gnome perched atop a pedestal bearing the word BILLIKEN, which Crazyboy feels sure must be connected to one of his favorite recordings from the 1920s, Texas Bill Day's "Billiken's Weary Blues." And on certain nights, as they walk into some ruin, greeted by the smells of lath and plaster and animal scat, he'll howl a line from that song into the gloom. *Don't your house look lonesome when your good girl is fixing to leave*—sometimes it sounds like an accusation, as if he already knows the doubts she won't let herself say out loud, but other times she can almost imagine a life with Crazyboy, see herself curled up next to him, not in some sad old house but in a nice clean new one. And increasingly, her sudden visions seem to be part of all that, pictures from the past and premonitions of the future rolled into one. She's never said a word about any of this to him—but every now and then, she'll get a feeling that the object of their search is close at hand, waiting for them in the dark.

Well, I may be right and I may be wrong
But it takes a worried woman to sing a worried song

And now she sees something inside that desk, a dull rectangular glimmer that makes her think of a precious little silver jewel box. Or maybe it's just her imagination playing tricks on her again, like the night she and Crazyboy came upon an old cast-iron pump hidden in the weeds. He grabbed the handle and began to swivel it, and she knelt down and cupped her hands beneath the spigot, almost as if she was praying. He worked faster and faster, skinny arms shooting up and down in a frenzy, just like now, T-shirt soaked with sweat, just like now. The sky turned silver, heat lightning flickering in the low gray clouds like some kind of coded message, some kind of sign. But nothing happened. Crazyboy kept ripping away and the pump kept shrieking, as if trying to fight him off, and finally he grew exhausted or disheartened (Meg never asked him) and they got in the car and drove home in silence. But this time she knows it's close, closer than it has been all summer. This time she can feel it rushing toward them, like clear, clean water rising up from the cold ground.

When a woman's in trouble, she wrings her hands and cries
But when a man's in trouble . . .

Gasping for breath in the thick air, he lowers the axe and

wipes his brow. Millions of dust motes flicker like little stars in the beam of Meg's flashlight, as if the whole universe is suddenly contained in this ramshackle room. And beyond them, that dim glow in the desk.

Crazyboy has inflicted so much damage that the thing now leans to one side, a staggered animal with a gaping wound. "Nothing there," he says, examining the hole.

But she pushes past him, thrusting her hand inside the shattered slats.

Part Two: 2014

This time she will find it inside a cardboard box that her stepmother sent from Joliet. The two women haven't seen each

other since the funeral for Meg's father five years ago, but every six months or so a package arrives at her home in Stony Brook, New York, with random mementos from the past. As an adult, Meg has sometimes known moments of genuine affection for her stepmother, but never love, and she is baffled both by the older woman's desire to maintain a bond that never quite existed and by her comically awkward way of reaching out. One package—filled with Meg's old shoes, including a right-footed hiking boot with no twin—included a sympathy card: *I'm so sorry to hear about your mother's death. She was a good woman, despite everything.* Another contained only her father's hearing aids in bubble wrap and a note: *We're the only ones left, Sweetie. Keep in touch. This latest box is topped with a pink Post-It: I cleaned out your desk.*

The contents include a Texas Instruments calculator (sticky to touch and missing buttons for the multiplication sign and the number three), five cones of still-fragrant sandalwood incense, a couple of miniature Dewar's bottles, both empty, and a ticket stub from a 1994 Willie Nelson concert that she cannot remember attending. Beneath those items, Meg will find her intermediate algebra textbook. And at the bottom of the box, she will come upon the postcard.

She has not seen William Fedorowicz, as everyone seems to call him now, since the summer after her sophomore year at the University of Chicago, when she ran into him at a party in their hometown. She had a new boyfriend by then, and she tried to be nice to William Fedorowicz, but William Fedorowicz, who was drunk as usual, called her a snob and grabbed her wrist and said he needed to talk to her outside. She pulled away and told him she planned to make something of herself. He said that she would never love anyone or anything as much as she loved him. She said if that turned out to be true, her life would be very tragic. Meg had learned to affect an ironic distance in college, and it made her giddy to unleash it now. She called him pathetic and ancient history, and when she was finished she realized people at the party were laughing at him. The next morning, her father shook her awake, furious that someone had scratched "WF" into the door of his new Acura.

Meg's old high school friends have told her that William Fedorowicz still lives in Joliet and, to everyone's surprise, has done well for himself—a pretty wife, a couple of cute kids, and a nice house in a subdivision. Meg laughed out loud when she heard that he makes his living selling home insurance, but she supposes he might find it equally amusing that she's an archaeologist.

She still snoops around old houses, only now they're from one of the world's first cities, built 5,000 years before the pharaohs started construction of the pyramids at Giza. The spring semester has just ended at Stony Brook University, and she has to turn her grades in so that she can get on a plane to Turkey, where she's doing research at the Neolithic site of Çatalhöyük in southern Anatolia. The people who lived there constructed no streets, cemeteries, or public gathering places. They built a honeycomb city, made from windowless mud-brick houses that had entryways cut into the roofs instead of front doors. After 1,400 years, they disappeared from history, leaving no written records.

Even after all this time in the profession, it still thrills her to tease soil from a delicate specimen with her trowel or to make a wall painting slowly appear by scraping away microscopic layers of plaster with a scalpel. It might take her and her colleagues six or seven years to excavate a single building, and if she sometimes flushes with guilt at the memory of ransacking those farmhouses with William Fedorowicz, she knows that in some fundamental way, she's still driven by the same impulse—crossing the divide of time to search for something lost, something missing, something that will make sense of everything else.

Over the years, however, she has grown skeptical that the fragmentary clues she and her colleagues spend their lives collecting will ever add up to a coherent narrative. More than ever, the past seems distant, unfathomable, open to interpretation. The people of Çatalhöyük buried their ancestors beneath the floor and slept on platforms above those corpses, as if they thought the dead could guide them through their daily lives. On days when she feels overwhelmed, Meg tries to imagine what messages her own father and mother might send her from beyond the grave. Nothing ever comes. As always, they can't be bothered, leaving her to figure things out for herself.

She's been married and divorced two times. Her first husband was an older archeologist, famous in the profession, who cheated on her from the start. The second was a colleague at Stony Brook, an unambitious, kindhearted sociologist, for whom she felt no passion. She had a miscarriage with each of these men. On most days, it feels like good fortune that she never had kids, at least as far as her career is concerned, and in any case it's too late to waste time on what might have been. She has her students to worry about, and her work. When she looks in the mirror now, she thinks of the plump, heavy-breasted female figurines often excavated at Çatalhöyük. She occasionally sleeps with another researcher there, a Turkish scholar with a wife and four children back in Istanbul. The sex is gentle, competent, collegial—two people obliging each other's need to be held. It always leaves her empty, but she will probably find herself with him again. Sometimes she has nightmares about a windowless house in a lost city, the ceiling door sealed shut, a pale glow rising from the opaque floor, lit from beneath by the luminescent blue corpse of a woman with no face. Other times she awakens to realize she's been dreaming about William Fedorowicz's eyes.

But she will not think about those eyes when she finds the postcard. She will not hear a soft voice singing *I went across the river and I lay down to sleep*. Instead, for the first time in more than twenty years, she will have one of those waking visions, more vivid than ever before: a porch on an autumn night, a bare-armed woman hugging herself against the chill, a car turning off a dark road and advancing up a long gravel drive, the headlamps just small dots at first but growing bigger, brighter, until the two beams merge, a blinding white light into which the woman now runs, arms open wide.

THE COMPLETE MIRACLES OF ST. ANTHONY

Definitive Edition with Previously Unpublished Material

The Miracle of the Fish

ANTHONY OF PADUA (1195–1231 CE), *Franciscan friar and priest. Venerated as the patron saint of lost and stolen items, he is credited with many miracles. On one occasion, the holy man went to preach in the Italian city of Rimini, which was then a hotbed of heresy. Local leaders had forbade the citizenry to pay him heed, however, and so all his attempts to lead sinners to the light of the veritable faith and the way of truth were met with silence. Frustrated by the obstinacy of the heretics, he decided to pray at a nearby place where the Marecchia River flows into the Adriatic Sea. There, inspired by God, he turned toward the water and called out, "Oh, you fish of the river and sea, hear now the Word of the Lord because the heretics do not desire to listen to it." At once thousands of fish stuck their heads above the surface and arranged themselves in neat rows, straining to hear each one of his words.*

At dawn, as police made plans to arrest Father Marek, a pilot whale washed up on a nearby beach. The priest himself was the first person to come upon the stranded animal, its sleek black skin glistening in the surf, its huge body writhing and flopping, its mouth pressed into what looked like a carefree smile.

Another passerby might have been alarmed by the discovery, but Father Marek's whole adult life had been a series of sudden arrivals and departures. His name, for instance, was a fabrication, though he had grown to like the sound of it on parishioners' lips. Nor was the priesthood his actual profession, though he had briefly studied at a seminary many years ago. His only occupation, one that took many forms, was convincing other people to place their trust in him. Standing over the beast while absentmindedly attempting to imitate its smile— an old habit he practiced on almost everyone he met—Father Marek thought about how much he'd enjoyed these past few months on Florida's Treasure Coast, how he'd miss these early morning strolls on the beach, when night and day were all one thing in the purple sky before sunrise.

Coming to a new place, starting a new life, inventing a new persona—all that was easy. Father Marek just drifted ashore and let people find him, exactly as this whale had done. One day he had shown up at the local parish in his robes, claiming to be a priest who had recently retired to Florida. He carried with him a commendatory letter from the bishop of the Diocese of New Ulm, Minnesota, and a kind of clerical ID card known as a *celebret*. Both of these documents were forgeries, of course, but the local pastor had barely glanced at them as he welcomed Father Marek into his church. Not only did the newcomer possess an easy knowledge of the particularities of celebrating Mass—how to put on vestments correctly, for instance, or how to flip to the correct pages of the missal— but with his unassuming manner, paunchy frame, jowly face, and sad blue eyes, he also had the air of someone you'd met before but couldn't quite place, someone who was too discreet to mention your lapse. Soon he was working as a substitute, or supply priest, in several local parishes, celebrating Mass, hearing confessions, organizing prayer meetings, officiating at weddings, and administering other sacraments as well as selling tickets, at $4,000 per person, for a pilgrimage to the Basilica of St. Anthony in Padua, Italy.

Making people believe his fabrications—Father Marek took no great pride in this talent, which was, after all, a fairly common one. His real genius, he knew, came in recognizing when their belief began to wane. That's what had always set him apart from other people who lived by their wits, what had kept him ahead of the law and, with the exception of seventeen unfortunate months in the Central Utah Correctional Facility, out of prison. And now, standing over the whale, he knew that unless he wanted to find himself in the same situation as that helpless animal, he would once again have to flee. On the previous night, the pastor of the local parish had called to invite him for coffee at the rectory in the morning. Most priests, he'd learned, were passable liars, but on this occasion Father Marek detected too much nonchalance in the other man's voice. Only a couple sentences into the conversation, he understood that his time here was at an end.

The whale lay on its side, staring up at him with a glassy, black eye, ancient and accusatory. What was that passage from Psalms 33—the one Father Marek had used in a recent homily?

Behold, the eye of the Lord is upon those who fear him,
upon those who count on his mercy,
To deliver their soul from death

The priest was far beyond worrying about his soul, and he feared arrest far more than he feared God. At least $60,000 remained of the money he'd collected for the pilgrimage, more than enough to make a new start. He had spent the night packing up his few worldly possessions, scrubbing down his motel room, throwing away anything that might later be used to tie him to this town, and wiping clean the hard drive of his laptop. Everything he owned was neatly packed into his car, a brand-new BMW that waited for him in the beach parking lot. To his own surprise, however, he was finding it hard to leave. It was not God's eye he felt upon him now but the gaze of someone who had strolled into the church a few weeks earlier, a woman whose name he had never learned, whose face he could barely remember, and whose whereabouts he did not know. Nonetheless, the thought of never seeing her again made him hesitate.

The sun was bursting open, a wound in the blood-colored horizon. Leaning over the whale, Father Marek saw his own shadow in its huge dark eye.

"There's nothing I can do for you," he said. "Please understand."

And then he hurried off, making sure, as he always did, to let the waves lap away his footprints as he disappeared down the shore.

The Miracle of the Drowned Child

In Lisbon, where the saint had received his early religious training and joined the Franciscan order, a group of boys pretending to be sailors once climbed into a boat and took it out on the waves. Suddenly, however, a violent storm broke loose, capsizing the vessel and casting the boys into the sea. All of them survived but one—a child who had not yet learned to swim. Upon hearing of the tragedy, the boy's mother rushed to the waterfront and begged the assistance of local fishermen, who lowered their nets and hauled up the lifeless body. The father of the drowned child wanted to hold a funeral right away, but the mother refused. "Either you leave him to me," she cried, "or you bury me with him!" Seeking out St. Anthony in tears, the desperate mother promised him that if the child was restored to her she would consecrate the boy to the Franciscan order. On the third day, her unceasing prayers were answered,

and the boy suddenly awoke as if from a deep sleep. When he grew up and became a Franciscan as promised, the young man took joy in telling his fellow friars how he had once drowned in the depths of the sea—and how God had brought him back to life through the intercession of St. Anthony.

It was one of those form-follows-function parish churches that had popped up all over the country in the last decades of the twentieth century—bare-brick interior, fan-shaped seating configuration, no-frills altar with an abstract, bloodless Jesus on the cross. The most notable feature of the place was a series of floor-to-ceiling stained-glass windows, rendered in a cartoonish style that must have seemed very modern when the church was built in 1974. Father Marek liked to think of them as a DC Comics version of The New Testament, with Superman as Jesus and Lex Luthor as Pontius Pilate. Each window came with its own cut-glass caption in vaguely psychedelic lettering—*The Beloved Disciple, The Rock* (for St. Peter), *The Betrayer* (for Judas), *The Pharisees*—as if the church was a giant biblical trading-card deck.

The first time he saw her, the woman was standing in front of the window depicting Mary Magdalene. The sun poured through the glass, leaving the stranger in shadows—achromatic, a mere outline beneath the words *The Witness*. The only feature he could make out was a dazzling corona of curly silver hair, unloosed either by humidity or lack of personal care, through which the colors of the window shimmered.

It was a Tuesday afternoon. The two of them were alone in the church, thirty feet apart. The place was silent, save for the steady whisper of air-conditioning vents. Although it was nearly one hundred degrees outside, Father Marek suddenly felt cold.

"May I help you?" he asked.

"Are you the priest?" replied the silhouetted figure. Even her voice seemed shadowy, full of absence.

Father Marek gestured to his collar, laughing. "Don't I look like one?"

The newcomer said nothing. He could feel her gaze upon him.

"Perhaps," he said, "you were expecting Father Guillermo, who is away for a meeting with the bishop. I'm the supply priest."

He stepped toward the visitor, trying to make out her face. "What can I do for you?" he asked.

Father Marek could now see that she was approximately his own age of fifty-five years. Thick but not plump, with a slumped bearing, a drawn look, and that wild cloud of silver hair, she struck him as being exhausted in some deep and fundamental way. Yet her brown eyes blazed, as if backlit like the windows. In her left hand, she cupped a small glass sphere, about the size of a baseball, which also somehow seemed to glow.

"I came here . . ." she said, then stopped in mid-sentence and stared down at the glass object for a few seconds, before looking up at him once more. "Can you tell me about St. Anthony?"

"You're not Catholic, I take it."

"My mother was Jewish. But I'm nothing."

"Well," he said, "Anthony of Padua is the patron saint of lost things."

Her eyes seemed to flare, but for a few seconds she was silent.

"Do you believe in miracles?" she finally asked.

"If I didn't believe in miracles," he said, "I guess I wouldn't be much of a priest."

He forced a laugh. She eyed him intently. In the cold of that room, the air thick with the smell of incense and new carpeting, he suddenly felt found out, seen.

"How do you know when it happens?" she said. "A miracle."

He glanced past her at the stained-glass image of a muscular Mary Magdalene, crouched before the Risen Christ like Wonder Woman ready to spring into action. During his Catholic-school upbringing, Father Marek had been taught that Mary Magdalene was a prostitute, but later, when he was studying to be a priest, he discovered that this detail of her life could be found nowhere in the Bible. It was just a story some pope had made up in the Middle Ages. And no one knew better than Father Marek that if you tell a story enough times with enough conviction, people are likely to believe it. Since coming to Florida, for instance, he'd been confiding to certain parishioners that, in addition to his pastoral duties, he was writing a book, *The Complete Miracles of St. Anthony: Definitive Edition with Previously Unpublished Material*. Such artifacts were important in his line of work. Like relics in the Catholic Church—a fragment of the true cross of Jesus, for example, or the mummified head of St. Catherine of Siena—they made even the most outlandish claims seem credible. That's why he'd pieced together more than two hundred typewritten pages of his nonexistent manuscript, which mostly consisted of stories copied from the internet or lifted from other books but also included miracles Father Marek had fabricated for his own amusement. If someone was on the fence about whether to shell out $4,000 for the pilgrimage, he'd usher that person aside and take out the book, which he would describe in hushed tones as his life's work. Then, after pledging the person to secrecy, he'd announce that at an obscure church archive in Padua, he had discovered a treasure trove of documents, including a beautifully illuminated manuscript from the fourteenth century, containing lost accounts of St. Anthony's miracles—miracles even more astonishing than any already known.

"Miracles," he told the woman, "are by their very nature difficult to describe."

"But isn't there some way of knowing? A sign?"

Many years of experience had taught Father Marek that the desire for miracles often made people even more vulnerable than the desire for money. But this woman, whose sad eyes studied him so intently, seemed somehow beyond his powers.

"Why do you ask these things?" he said.

She stared at him, then gazed down once more at that little glass object, as if it were a crystal ball in which she was searching for a clue. For an instant, he thought she might turn and leave—a possibility that, to his surprise, made him bristle with regret. But then, with the grim resignation of someone who must leap from the window of a burning house, she threw herself into a story. In a breathless flurry of words, she told him how twenty years ago her son had vanished from a nearby beach while surfing, how no clues had ever been found, how she and her husband had begun returning every year, how they'd spent more than a decade collecting objects from the surf, bringing them back home to Michigan, studying them, arranging them in different configurations, as if those random bits of wreckage were the untranslated hieroglyphs of some secret language that might help them understand their loss. "It was insanity," she said. "We knew that from the start, but it took years to stop. We finally managed to promise each other that we'd never come back here, that we'd put the place out of our minds."

"And now?" he said.

"My husband died two months ago," she replied. "And somehow with him gone, I couldn't stop myself. I've been roaming the beach for these last three days."

"And you found something, I suppose," he said. "Something miraculous."

His sudden contempt for her was comforting—the familiar mix of disgust and disdain that he always felt for those who allow themselves to be deceived. For a moment, it seemed that the strange anxiety he'd been experiencing ever since she arrived was at last lifting. Then she held out the glass ball.

Taking it in his hands, he saw that it was something like a snow globe, only without the snow. On its base were the words *St. Anthony*. Holding the object up to the stained glass,

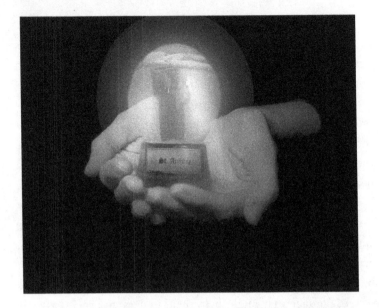

which gave it an oddly bluish glow, Father Marek saw that it held a figurine—a man with a tonsure haircut and the brown habit of a Franciscan friar. Striding through the murky fluid inside the globe, as if making his way back to shore, the tiny saint was holding a child.

With a hushed sputter, the air conditioning went silent. Not wanting to meet the woman's eyes, Father Marek studied the sphere for a long time in that still room. What were the odds that such a fragile antique would survive the ravages of the sea? A pair of unsettling possibilities—that something other than happenstance had brought this object to the beach, and that something other than happenstance had brought this woman to his church—shot through his mind. Then came an even more troubling thought—that the woman had fabricated the story for her own aims, as yet unclear, and that she was now roping in Father Marek, not the other way around.

"By a curious coincidence," he finally said, "I happen to be organizing a pilgrimage to St. Anthony's holy shrine in Italy."

She was still staring at him, unblinking, her face intense, indecipherable.

"I have some pamphlets in my office," he said. "Let me get you one."

But when he came back, she was gone.

The Miracle of the Tongue

Moments before he was taken from the world at age thirty-six, St. Anthony was heard to say, "I see the Lord." It is recorded that at the precise moment of his death on June 13, 1231, children spontaneously ran into the streets weeping, and church

bells rang of their own accord. When his body was exhumed thirty-two years later, it was found to be entirely decomposed except for the tongue, which was still "beautiful, fresh and ruby red," according to one eyewitness. This divine favor, it is believed, was a sign from God to let future generations know that St. Anthony never once failed to speak the truth.

After departing from the whale, Father Marek continued down the shore, pants rolled up, wingtip shoes dangling from one hand, bare feet slapping at the surf, thoughts racing. He'd always been as amorphous as the ocean, adapting himself to the peculiar shapes of other people's dreams, and when the time came he would simply wash away, a wave sliding under the surface, nothing in its wake but a fleeting shimmer. Now it was time to disappear once more—his escape from arrest, he knew, depended on decisive action—yet he couldn't quite resist a few more minutes by the sea. Glancing back at that stranded beast, he made a bargain with himself. Whenever it disappeared from view, he would rush to his car and drive away forever. But every time he turned around, he could still see its silhouette, not much smaller than the last time he'd looked. Wondering if it was an optical illusion, he cupped both hands around his eyes to block the rising sun and squinted up the waterline. The whale was still in sight, shining like a black glass bead, though it no longer seemed to be moving. Had it died in those few minutes since he left? Father Marek remembered a video he had once seen—the carcass of a sperm whale suddenly exploding due to a buildup of methane gas from the decomposition of its internal organs. The skin ripping open, the guts blasting out, the blood cascading from inside like a crashing wave— even now, the thought of it filled him with revulsion. Ever since he could remember, he'd been disgusted by body parts, blood, entrails—things that should be kept internal and intact, separate from the exterior self.

Back in seminary, he'd traveled with a group of fellow students from Chicago to Italy to see the preserved tongue of St. Anthony—an experience that caused him to abandon plans for the priesthood. February 15, 1981: He recalled the exact date because he was one of thousands of devotees in Padua that day for the Feast of the Translation of the Saint's Relics, commonly known as the Feast of the Tongue. What he remembered about the chapel all these years later were the dozens of white marble angels, gaudy fantasies of the baroque period, frolicking playfully above the main altar. He remembered the smirks on their faces, as if they were staring down with contempt at the endless line of gullible humans waiting to venerate the tongue. He remembered his own revulsion at being brushed against and breathed upon by his fellow pilgrims, his disgust with the sickly smells of their perfumes and colognes, the cigarette smoke in their clothes, the stink of their unwashed bodies, the desperate hopes and fears that seemed to rise out of them like the bacterial reek of a putrid wound. He remembered their ridiculous carryings-on at the ornate gold case in which the tongue was housed—the tears and prayers and signings of the cross, the kissing and touching of the glass cabinet containing the reliquary, the whispering and moaning and comically exaggerated gesturing. And, of course, he remembered his own encounter with the tongue—how it had seemed like nothing more than a triangular glob of pickled gray flesh, how it had left him empty of emotion, how it had given him no comfort, only a furious surge of nausea, and how, catching the sight of his own reflection in that filthy glass cabinet, he had realized he wore the same sneering grin as those marble angels overhead. And it was then that he knew the truth—not just that he could never be a priest, but that being a priest was the most pathetic and preposterous thing he could ever dream of becoming.

He'd felt dizzy, stomach acid swelling in his throat. Near the altar was a spot where pilgrims could write prayers to St. Anthony and stuff them in a box. Almost instinctively, Father Marek reached into his breast pocket and pulled out something he'd scribbled on a piece of hotel stationary that morning. Then he hesitated. What was the use? Why even bother going through the motions? A line formed behind him, fellow worshippers staring at him and whispering angrily in various languages. Stifling the urge to throw up, he slid the note into the slot.

> O Holy St. Anthony gentlest of Saints, your love for God and charity for His creatures, made you worthy, when on earth, to possess miraculous powers. Encouraged by this thought, I implore you to help me find my father, Steven Dabrowski Sr., who abandoned my mother in Chicago when I was seven years old and has never returned or attempted to contact me, his only child.
>
> O gentle and loving St. Anthony, whose heart was ever full of human sympathy, whisper my petition into the ears of the sweet Infant Jesus, who loved to be folded in your arms. The gratitude of my heart will ever be yours. Amen.

Fifteen years later, Father Marek would solve the mystery of his biological father—not through the intercession of St. Anthony, nor through any of his usual clandestine means, but through one of those new genealogy databases that appeared in the mid-1990s. It was all too easy. Set up an account, type in your name and date of birth, and learn that the man you've been seeking your whole life is dead. Search the database some more and discover that after abandoning you and your mom, he moved ninety miles north to Milwaukee, where he got work as a machinist, the same job he'd had in Chicago. Do a few additional internet searches and find out he served three years for forgery in a check-fraud scheme, drifted in and out of at least two other marriages, and had one additional child, a son two years younger than you. Send that half brother an email asking him if he wants to meet to talk about the old man. When he doesn't respond, steal his identity and purchase several expensive suits on his credit card.

Turning anger into opportunity—that was Father Marek's secret to success. While other people wallowed in unpleasant feelings, he transformed them into hard cash. Take that long-ago debacle in Italy, for example. Disagreeable as it may have been at the time, the experience had nonetheless provided him with the know-how needed to convince more than forty parishioners that he would arrange every small detail of their pilgrimage—roundtrip airfare to Padua, lodging at the Hotel Donatello on Via Del Santo, a private tour of the Basilica with Father Marek's good friend, the nonexistent Friar Mario Segreti, and, for a select few, a glimpse of that rare illuminated manuscript containing lost miracles of St. Anthony—all in return for an affordable flat-rate fee, payable by cash, check, crypto, or direct deposit to the priest's checking account.

Incarnare: Latin for "to make flesh." Father Marek had read somewhere that a person's body contains about twenty different chemical elements, the products of supernova explosions that scattered ancient stars. But the human husk—that wasn't formed from oxygen, carbon, hydrogen, nitrogen, all those meaningless atoms, but from words. That's how he had reincarnated himself over and over—telling stories that others believed, *wanted* to believe, *needed* to believe in order to justify their own stories, make their own flesh. During decades of shifting personas—financial consultant, IRS agent, attorney, dealer of rare coins, cancer researcher, decorated war veteran, English professor, priest—Father Marek had begun to take for granted that his whole being consisted of words, that he was more or less incorporeal. And so, in the days after his encounter with that woman at the church, it was disconcerting to find himself full of weight and sensation, pained by an ache he couldn't quite name, or perhaps not an ache but a kind of constant rawness, or perhaps not either of those things but a sensation of being exposed.

Yes, exposed, like St. Anthony's tongue in its glass display case—when Father Marek had stood before the congregation five days after the woman's sudden appearance, he found himself fumbling for words, forgetting the order of things, feeling at a loss about how to look and act. Glancing up from his homily, he thought he saw her standing at the back of the church, her hair filled with light, her face lost in darkness, but when he blinked she was gone. There and not there—an apparition. The Complete Miracles of St. Anthony was full of such phantoms—a dead man who came back to life to identify his murderer; the Baby Jesus who suddenly appeared in the saint's arms; the saint himself who more than four hundred years after his own death showed up in the little Polish village of Radecznica to request that a shrine be built on a nearby hill. There and not there—hadn't that always been Father Marek's own power over everyone else? So why was he suddenly the one haunted by these visions? There and not there in the church, there and not there as he lay sleepless in his empty and silent motel room, there and not there as she slowly turned to him on this beach, her feet ankle-deep in the surf, her face still in shadows—and then she reached out to him, and then she vanished once more, just another inexplicable hallucination, the result, perhaps, of the stress and confusion of his unplanned departure. Breathless, he wheeled to look for the whale, half expecting it to be gone, too, but there it was, shimmering in the distance like a phantasm from some dream, some mystical reverie, some confidence trick of the mind.

The Miracle of the Lost Coin

In 1621, a Bavarian nobleman, traveling from Warsaw to Ingolstadt, rested for the evening in the city of Pilsen, where, *during a long night of carousing, he misplaced a gift he had just received from Sigismund III Vasa, King of Poland—a gold coin worth the astonishing sum of one hundred ducats. The innkeeper urged him to seek the assistance of St. Anthony by having a mass said at the nearby Franciscan church, but the nobleman ignored this plea. For three days and three nights, he searched desperately for the coin, a fantastic rarity minted specially to mark the Catholic victory over the infidel Turks at the Battle of Chocim, where thousands of unbelievers were slaughtered. At last, the despondent traveler abandoned his efforts and left the city, never to return. As the years wore on, he grew more and more embittered until at last his faith*

waned entirely. By the time his travels took him to Padua, he was an old man. While touring the town, he heard so much about the miracles of Saint Anthony that he decided to visit the renowned Basilica del Santo. Simple curiosity took him through those doors, but once inside he found himself stand-ing in the chapel under which the holy body of the saint lay, which caused him to reflect on the necessity of saving his own soul. Repenting his past apostasy, he left the sanctuary in a kind of trance and began wandering the streets. Many hours passed. At dusk, on a little-traversed passageway near the city wall, he noticed a glimmer at his feet. Wedged between two cobblestones was the same coin he had lost in Pilsen—one of only ten ever minted.

Father Marek had made up "The Miracle of the Lost Coin" as a kind of inside joke that only he and his past selves would understand. He'd learned about King Sigismund's one hun-dred-ducat piece—one of the rarest and most valuable ever minted in history—during his days as a cigar-smoking, Brooks Brothers-wearing numismatic dealer who convinced dozens of collectors across the country to wire him money, promis-ing them an inside line on obtaining gold coins below market value. That particular chapter in his life, alas, had come to an abrupt end just before the completion of an extremely lucra-tive transaction. And while Father Marek was relieved to have once again slipped away just before the authorities closed in, the thought of leaving so much money on the table had irri-tated him ever since—thus, the "lost coin" of his parable.

But what came to mind now, as he stumbled up that beach, was not the glistening coin but the man wandering in a trance. Yes, trance. What else to call this confusion, this indecision, this undoing of time? Although he knew better than to be swept up in his own fictions, least of all one he'd made up on a lark after several glasses of bourbon, Father Marek couldn't shake the idea that "The Miracle of the Lost Coin" somehow foretold his own fate. Not that he repented. No, never. To repent would be to look back, and to look back would be to lose his gift for reincarnation. All the same, he couldn't help feeling a sense of rupture, almost imperceptible, a door opening faintly somewhere, an unfamiliar emotion sweeping in, something like hope but also something like remorse. And standing at that door was the woman with wild silver hair.

There and not there and then there again. At the church two days earlier, she'd suddenly reappeared a few feet from him.

"How," she asked, "do I go about making a confession?"

They were standing in the vestibule, its walls lined with stained-glass windows depicting the Parables of Jesus. Just over her shoulder was *The Anointer*, a woman crouched next to the seated Jesus as she washed his feet. Father Marek studied his visitor. She looked tired, haggard, a defeated woman on the downside of middle age, yet suddenly he wanted to reach out and caress her face. Such an unfamiliar desire, so different from his hunger for prostitutes or his hunger for people with possessions he might make his own—for an instant, he was tempted to come clean, reveal that he was not what he appeared to be. Instead, he led her to the confessional, showed her how to make the sign of the cross, and taught her to say "Bless me, Father, for I have sinned."

Kneeling in the booth next to him, she was silent for a long time. Then she leaned over and took something out of her purse.

"To love the child who is gone and feel nothing for the one who is there—surely that must be unforgivable in the eyes of God," she said.

She was now cupping something in her hands, something

that gave off a dull glow—the glass ball she had brought to the church during her last visit. Choosing her words slowly, she seemed to be speaking less to him than to the tiny figure inside the globe.

"I have a daughter," she said. "She was only nine when my boy vanished. Blameless, perfectly blameless. She wasn't even there. I haven't spoken to her in at least a year. She's in New Orleans; I'm not sure I even have an address. Her twenty-fourth birthday was two months back. My fault, the whole thing. This won't make sense to you, but since the day he disappeared, I've been stuck on an endless shore. Sometimes I have this waking dream of a distant rectangle, a sort of square arch rising from the water's edge like an entranceway. It aways fades as fast as it arrives, this vision or hallucination or who knows what, but each time it happens I'm more sure than ever that he's just on the other side, waiting for me."

Father Marek remembered a story, famous in his line of work, about a psychic who once convinced a grieving mother to turn over $17 million by promising to transfer the soul of her dead son into another boy's body. Such a stupid woman, so deserving of her fate. He wanted to feel the same contempt for the person kneeling next to him but couldn't, wanted to console her but didn't know how, wanted to speak to her but had no words, wanted to have a small fraction of her faith in God, or in the ocean, or in whatever it was that she thought was sending her messages, wanted to want anything on earth as much as she wanted to be with her dead son. She drew a long breath and told him that many years ago she'd wandered into the sea one morning with no intention of turning back. It was a foggy day, she said, the kind when water and land are hard to tell apart, which somehow made it seem easier to finally leave one for the other.

"I kept walking until I was totally, you know, beneath. My

husband was in a panic on the shore, shouting my name. But that's not what stopped me."

"What was it, then?" Father Marek heard himself saying.

She studied the glass ball.

"Something happened, I don't know. A revelation, I guess you'd call it."

"Revelation?"

"Yes," she said, staring into the globe. "I thought that if my son needed me, he'd send me a sign. One that couldn't be mistaken."

Father Marek imagined himself running through the surf in a fog, wrapping his arms around her waist, pulling her from the waves.

"What do we do now?" she said.

"Now?"

"In the confession. What comes next?"

His mind raced through the order of the sacrament—penance, contrition, absolution—but he couldn't remember the words for any of it. He found himself whispering, "Come away with me. Join me on my pilgrimage."

"What are you saying?"

"We'll go to Italy," he said. "Don't let money be an obstacle. I'll take care of everything. We'll visit the Basilica of St. Anthony and pray for the lost."

"No. Impossible. I don't understand."

"But don't you see? It's God's wish. That's why you found that thing on the beach. That's the meaning in all this. You're being called to St. Anthony's shrine."

She did not speak, did not move, did not even seem to breathe.

"No," she replied at last. "That's not where I'm being called."

Putting the glass ball back into her purse, she said nothing.

Through the latticework of the grille, he watched her leave, a silhouette slowly losing form, a wave folding itself into the sea.

The Miracle of Her

During his sojourn at the Franciscan monastery at Montpellier, St. Anthony was visited by a man who had led a very bad and profligate life. Throwing himself at the holy man's feet, the stranger begged to be reunited with a woman whom he had once seen praying in a church. When the saint inquired about why this sinner

He never finished writing that last miracle. Time was running out and he couldn't find the words. Why had he wasted his last few minutes at the motel trying to figure out how the parable would end? And why was he still on this beach now, knowing that each second of delay lessened his chances of escape? He felt he had been here for hours, the waves lulling him into a stupor. Looking back, he saw that whale was still there, a radiant object in the distance. And then, turning and glancing ahead again, he noticed another radiant object.

A glass ball. Or something that looked like a glass ball—a bottle, maybe, catching the light at an odd angle. He took a couple of steps, stopped, watched it dazzle in the surf, a light so intense it brought to mind that passage from Ezekiel when the prophet sees a ball of fire with "a brilliance like that of amber" before hearing the voice of God. Father Marek scanned the water, half expecting to spot the woman, waist-deep, glancing back before disappearing beneath the waves. Picturing a corpse on the beach, just around the next curve, he felt a shudder of revulsion or perhaps of fear. But maybe she hadn't gone

through with it. Maybe she was still alive. Maybe he could find her. And then he was running—not toward the shiny thing but in the other direction, tossing off his shoes as he hurried up the shore, already winded, already soaked with sweat. He felt heavy and weightless at once, as if his legs were filled with sand, his feet only touching the ground every few steps. Suddenly, he found himself standing over the whale.

Still on its side, the beast lay still, its eye now shut. "I'm sorry," Father Marek said, gasping for breath as he leaned over the body. "There was really nothing I could do." And then he had his hands out to push, not knowing why, but pushing with all his strength. The whale didn't move, didn't stir. He felt certain it was dead, but he kept pushing anyway, determined to reunite it with the ocean. Such an absurdity. Such a useless, farcical waste of time, but he didn't stop, couldn't stop. Tearing off his shirt, he tried to wrap his arms around the whale, lowering his shoulder into its cool skin and pushing furiously, grunting and screaming until his feet slipped in the sand and he fell to his knees, landing face first on the beast's bulbous head. Suddenly, the eye blinked open, a glassy, black globe inside of which blazed a rectangle of golden light. And inside that gleam, Father Marek could barely make out the reflection of a man, stooped like a humble penitent in prayer, the sound of a distant police siren drifting across the beach.

WHY I MARRIED MY WIFE

My wife, who has an unlabored comfort with the world that I admire (except in those moments when I despise it), teases me that I am never capable of leaving well enough alone. Whether she's right is of no consequence to this story, but I will concede that most men in my situation that day, pissing along some muddy Indiana roadside, would have just zipped up their pants and climbed back into their cars, instead of wandering, as I did, farther out into the weeds. What had caught my attention were the crows, hundreds of them, crowded into a lone cottonwood at the edge of a soybean field, as though they might all fly off at once and take the tree with them, black soil raining down from the exposed roots. In the dull heat, those birds seemed strangely agitated, cawing at each other in peevish tones, some pacing the branches, others flapping noisily from perch to perch, their iridescent wings shimmering in the late afternoon sun. The cause of their fury, it appeared, was something in the gully between their tree and the place where I stood. Every few seconds, one of them would fly low over the weeds, circling and recircling with steady rowing wing strokes, before returning with a throaty report to its comrades in the branches.

I can't recall what I was thinking about just then, other than how I wished I had taken my hay fever medicine. The air clung to my nostrils as stubbornly as the thistles stuck to my pants while I made my way down that incline. It had rained the night before, so I found myself sliding with every few steps, ruining a pair of new Italian shoes and barely managing to remain on my feet. At the bottom, among the cattails, was the sort of improvised junkyard you sometimes find along country lanes: several cracked toilet bowls; random piles of old bricks and asphalt; a half-charred wooden picnic table; a rolltop desk that looked like somebody had taken a hatchet to it; and the rusted chassis of a DeSoto, two empty miniature bottles of Dewar's standing neatly on the dashboard behind a shattered windshield. Wondering why I had ever abandoned my air-conditioned car, I turned to leave, but starting back up the hill I happened to notice an odd gleam from behind the remains of a sofa. Lying in the weeds, as if someone had just put it there for safe keeping, was a motorcycle, chrome freshly polished, keys in the ignition, scent of gasoline still lingering in the air. As I crouched over it, the calls from the tree grew more ecstatic. And then, amid the din of the crows, I heard a moan.

He was more a carcass than a person by then. He had apparently been wearing neither a shirt nor a safety helmet when he slid off the road, and now his neck, back, and bald head were crisscrossed with scrapes and gashes. A crescent-shaped wound under his left shoulder blade was so deep that a couple of his ribs were in plain view. His skin, where it was still intact, was a horrible shade of crimson; he must have been face down in the sun that whole day, perhaps longer. His arms and legs floated limp at his side while his wide frame sagged into the mud like some great burst blister, making it hard to distinguish where his battered skin left off and the ground began. He smelled of his own shit.

I would have been relieved to find him dead, but he was still breathing, if just barely, a faltering arid hiss. His large shaved head, kinked so violently to the side that it almost seemed disconnected from his body, was varnished with blood and sweat, giving his skin the color and appearance of uncooked chicken. An eye flitted at mine as I approached, then rolled back into his skull.

"Can you hear me?" I said.

Putting his parched lips together, he seemed to whisper something. I squatted over him and leaned close. I can't remember touching him, but when I looked down there was blood on my fingers.

"I can't understand you," I said. "What are you trying to say?"

"Tell my brother," he rasped, with unexpected loudness. "Tell him he can find what he's looking for out at Demerest Lake."

"Don't worry about that," I said, wishing I hadn't left my cell phone back at the car. "You're going to be fine, OK?"

"Demerest Lake. On the north shore. By the big willow tree. Tell him."

"Yes, sure. Demerest. But you should try to stay calm."

He didn't respond, and so after a while I left him, promising to fetch some water and call for help. It took me a number of attempts to climb that muddy hillside. By the time I finally called for an ambulance, the crows had begun to alight on his back.

* * *

Not a whole lot had been asked of me until that moment. I had never been married, never had children, never been divorced, never been sued or imprisoned or stabbed or shot or addicted, never been to war, never hated or been hated, never experienced the death of someone I truly loved. I prided myself on doing right but was aware that the task had, until very recently, required little effort or sacrifice. I had a few good friends, a supportive family, a more than adequate income. I lived with an amiable and attractive woman (though not the one I would soon marry), whom my parents and siblings adored (unlike the one I would soon marry). In these things, I had always considered myself lucky, but at thirty-three years of age, I was starting to feel not so much blessed as passed by. It occurred to me that while I made my living selling medical supplies—everything that cuts, clamps, stitches, monitors, measures, or probes the human body—my own hands had never been covered with someone else's blood until just now. What had happened in that gully, I realized as I watched a police car move toward me from far up the road, was easily the most memorable event of my life.

"It's Kirby Jussel," said the county sheriff's officer as we sloshed our way downhill. "Don't even need to see the body. That's his bike."

I was due in Terre Haute for a sales conference the next morning but had already determined to miss it, if necessary. I had made a promise to the dead man, and, besides, my curiosity was aroused. They would just have to do without me.

The county sheriff's officer, a tall man with the smooth face of a twelve-year-old and the sandy voice of a geezer, appeared to know the victim well but seemed neither surprised nor saddened by his demise. "Bound to happen sooner or later," he said, squatting down and lifting the dead man's head by its shaggy gray beard. "Yeah, that's Kirby all right. When I wasn't ticketing this guy for speeding, I was busting him for drugs or for taking target practice on some 4-H kid's pet goats. They took away his license a bunch of times, even sent him to the state pen once—never stopped him. Dude was wacko."

I asked him whether Kirby Jussel had any brothers in the area. He laughed and let the chin plop back into the mud.

"Well, there's his twin, Roy. That's his only brother."

"He asked me to give him a message."

The county sheriff's officer seemed to find this notion both absurd and amusing. "Let me guess," he said with a gruff chuckle. "Dear bro: Get yourself straight to hell."

Roy Jussel lived off a winding blacktop that had been potholed and patched so many times it seemed less like a road than an ancient geological feature, an asphalt outcropping left behind by the retreat of some primal sea. His house, a sagging Victorian in need of new paint and a new roof, was once the centerpiece of a family farm that, like so many others in the area, had been swallowed up by one of its large-scale competitors. Now it stood on a small plot, fenced off from the surrounding cornfields, all vestiges of its former glory gone, save for a gap-toothed windmill whimpering with each lopsided revolution. Still, the lawn was thick and neatly trimmed, the garden lush with just-ripe tomatoes. On the front porch, toy cars and trucks rested in parking-lot-perfect rows. The floorboards, warped and worn, had been mopped so recently the smell of synthetic lemon still hung in the air. I was on the road four days a week back then and had driven past hundreds of old places like this. Cut off from the farms that gave them purpose, they sometimes fell apart so fast it made you wonder if a building could have a death wish. But despite its decrepitude, this place seemed different. Perhaps it was because of the dusk, the way it can make a building look so tranquil, but as I walked across that porch, I felt a shiver of envy for Roy Jussel.

He was standing on the other side of the screen door. With his thick black hair, clean-shaven face, and athletic build, he looked years younger than his twin. Nonetheless, you could tell the two were brothers: same big head, same Roman nose, same deep-set eyes. He greeted me by name, explaining that the county sheriff's officer, calling to deliver the bad news, had mentioned that I might visit. Although he thanked me for coming all the way out to his place, he did not open the door. I told him what little I could about the circumstances of his brother's death and described how I had happened upon the accident scene. Then I blurted out Kirby's last words.

He nodded grimly but showed no other outward signs of emotion. "Well," he said, "I suppose I'll have to go out there first thing in the morning."

There was nothing left to say. I did not leave. I was hoping, I suppose, that Jussel would invite me inside. In the back of my mind, I thought that he owed me that much, or at least that he owed me some explanation of his brother's message. So I stood my ground, scrounging for conversation. We talked about the thunderstorms that were expected at the end of the week. We talked about the St. Louis Cardinals and their need for relief pitching. We talked about pickup trucks, the model I should buy if I ever needed one. And as strange as it may sound, I think he appreciated the company and the distraction. His wife and their four children, he explained, were visiting relatives in Ohio and would not be home until the following afternoon. Still, he kept the screen door shut.

I would not describe Roy Jussel as a handsome man, but he had vibrant green eyes that gave warmth to an otherwise inexpressive face. I cannot remember seeing him smile or laugh, though he sometimes responded to my small talk with a smirk that suggested considerable intelligence and humor. Moderate in speech and dress, he had one glaring eccentricity, which I did not notice until I had been looking at him through that wire mesh for almost fifteen minutes. Wrapped loosely around his left hand and forearm was a threadbare piece of satin, once colored blue, or perhaps lavender, but now faded to a vaguely pastelish gray. He was stroking it softly with the fingertips of his other hand.

He noticed my look of curiosity. "Believe it or not," he said, "you're watching a grown man snuggle with his child-hood security blanket. I don't use it much—only during emer-gencies, really—but I'm not ashamed to tell you that it gives me a great deal of comfort."

Jussel made this peculiar declaration with such disarming glibness I found myself at a loss for words. "It must be dif-ficult," I finally mumbled. "I can't imagine losing a brother."

He watched his right hand as it passed lightly over the satin. "Kirby and I used to share this blanket. We shared a lot of things, but that is too long a story," he said.

And then he excused himself and closed the door, leaving me alone on that porch to sneeze amid the last rays of the sun and the first glimmer of fireflies across the fields.

I had not eaten since breakfast. Twelve miles from Jussel's place stood a diner, its roof adorned by a giant fiberglass steer so faded by decades of sun that, pale, white-eyed, and lit from beneath, it looked like some pagan deity set down on the out-skirts of Dugger, Indiana. The dining room was small and smelled of meat and steamed broccoli. Its florescent lighting was merciless, the whole scene from an overexposed photo-graph. Chrome glistened on 1950s-era appliances. The place was crowded, but it took me a moment to realize that almost everyone there was involved in the same conversation.

"If you ask me, Roy shares in the blame for this. You don't do to a brother what he did to Kirby," said a plump woman near the windows.

"All's fair in love and war," said a sunburned man across the room. "And anyway, Kirby got his revenge, and then some."

"That's just a rumor," said an old fellow in short sleeves and a necktie.

"Give me a break," said the sunburned man. "Does anyone here sincerely believe what happened to Roy was an accident?"

I took a seat at the counter and ordered soup and coffee, my back to the room. Opposite me was a mirror-lined pastry case, and if I peered over the strawberry-rhubarb and gooseberry pies, I could watch the other patrons. It was difficult to make sense of what they were saying, in part because they spoke in a kind of abbreviated patter, the natural result of everyone in the room knowing almost everything there was to know about everyone else, and in part because the main discussion often spun off into smaller conversations, the threads of which were impossible to follow at once. Nor did they seem inclined to provide background for the only stranger present. On the few occasions that I ventured questions to the group, I was met with such suspicious looks and guarded answers that I quickly gave up. The only person inclined to talk with me was the waitress, a redhead who had graduated high school with the Jussel brothers. She had gone to college in Muncie, she told me, but now found herself "stuck back in this shit town." Perhaps she saw me as a fellow outsider, or perhaps she appreciated the dollar tips I stacked on the counter whenever she refilled my coffee. She was, in any case, willing to fill in the gaps as I struggled to make sense of the story.

The Jussel family came to Indiana from the mountains of East Tennessee. There, the boys' fraternal grandparents had apparently been members of a Pentecostal sect that practiced snake handling. As an adult, Kirby Jussel was said to have taken perverse pleasure in showing friends a faded black-and-white photograph of his grandmother as a young woman, a thick rattlesnake draped sensuously around her neck, an ecstatic look on her face. Some of my fellow patrons claimed the boys' parents had abandoned the more extreme trappings of their faith after moving to Indiana, but no one disputed that Kirby and Roy grew up in a strict home, where tobacco, caffeine, and alcohol were shunned as devils and leather belts were embraced as great preachers.

"They used to dress those boys in matching outfits," said an older woman, "but not because they thought it was cute. They just believed clothing should be simple: ostentation was a sin. I think Roy and Kirby were only ever allowed a few toys, and even then it was one bike for both kids, one baseball glove for both kids, and so on. They treated them almost like they were the same child."

The trouble, everyone seemed to agree, was that the Jussel boys never were the same. Kirby was a good student; Roy got straight A's. Kirby tried hard to ingratiate himself to others; Roy was elected class president. Kirby was a fine high school athlete; Roy was an all-state pitcher whose powerful left arm landed him a scholarship at Indiana University and then a minor-league baseball contract.

"Still, you never saw them apart, at least not until after high school," explained my waitress. "Then it was like they went in opposite directions."

Exposed to new influences and ideas at college, Roy rejected his fundamentalist upbringing. Kirby did not abandon the faith per se, but he did flee his parents' home and their rules. Dropping out of the local junior college, he moved into a house in the country with some people he barely knew, coworkers at a factory that produced plastic cups.

"That's where he started getting into everything he'd been denied," said the waitress. "All of sudden he was the king of the hell-raisers. Maybe it ended up killing him, but for a while he was lots of fun. He really did have a lot of charisma, that guy. It's like he figured out that if he couldn't be his brother, he could at least be the life of every last party."

And so it happened that Roy Jussel, professional baseball player and pride of the whole community, came home one day to find the tables turned: Kirby finally had something that he coveted. Her name was Emily.

"Kirby loved that girl dearly," said my waitress. "And she loved Kirby, too, I think. Until . . ."

"Ain't right what Roy did to Kirby," said the plump woman.

"Ain't right what Kirby did to him," repeated the sun-burned man.

"That's a rumor, nothing more," declared the old man in short sleeves and a necktie. "And it doesn't bear repeating right now."

As he said this, he turned to me with an accusing nod, so as to remind the others that a nosy intruder was in their midst. In the mirror, I watched them watching me, and as I studied those unfamiliar and unfriendly faces, my mind began to race over all the other restaurants where I had dined alone, all the towns I had passed through anonymously. And suddenly, I hated those people for their rooted past and common frame of reference.

They could keep their secrets. I had one of my own.

"I heard another rumor," I said, rising to my feet with an affected yawn and tossing down some more bills. "I heard that a passerby, some traveling salesman, came upon Kirby before he died. I heard Kirby gave that man a message to deliver to Roy. I heard he's the only person in this whole town who knows what passed between them."

Then I strolled out into the parking lot and climbed into my car. A half mile away, I turned sharply off the road and bounded into a fallow field, Queen Anne's lace and cockleburs and sour dock enveloping the headlights. Climbing into the back seat, I lapsed into a fitful sleep, a full moon in the sky and a ghostly white bull on the horizon.

* * *

My wife was then the wife of another man, a surgeon, one of my longtime customers. They spent most of their hours together—she managed his office—but their physical proximity had not guaranteed an emotional closeness. Jane is an open and impulsive person, a woman who finds more joy in the world than most people but who does not run from sorrow. Her ex-husband, a talented but uncommunicative man, loved her for these qualities at first, no doubt, but later found them to distract from his focus on work and golf. They had been cursed by a miscarriage early on and later invested huge amounts of time and money in ever more technologically complex and spiritually devastating attempts at parenthood. He did not particularly like children, according to my wife, but that did not stop him from blaming her, silently, for failing to provide one. She blamed him too—for his silence, for his lack of empathy, for not loving her all the more because of their struggles. The pursuit of a baby had been their main topic of conversation for so many years that when they finally abandoned that pursuit they had no idea what to say to each other. It was about then that she and I began our long, strange flirtation.

I liked her, at first, because she seemed exotic. On the day I met her, she was wearing a loop of eight-millimeter film around her neck like a choker; it was, she explained, her favorite scene from a Buster Keaton movie, "the one where the whole house crashes down around him, but he barely takes notice." Such flamboyant tastes might not have stood out at an art gallery, but at a doctor's office in suburban Indianapolis it seemed truly subversive, as did her chaotic energy and convulsive laughter. I liked her because she appeared to be as dissatisfied in her world as I was beginning to feel in mine. I liked her because I suspected (correctly, it turned out) that she was intensely passionate and loving. I liked her because of the attention she paid me. And although I was not aware of it at the time, I liked her because she was married to someone else and therefore out of reach.

Our friendship developed slowly but then intensified with a force that surprised me, even though it had been largely at my instigation. For several years I had taken her out to lunch every three or four months to discuss business, but at some point I started to find more excuses for these meetings, and the conversations drifted further and further from medical supplies. We began a correspondence by email and text. On the road, I would check my phone compulsively for word from her; sometimes we would write back and forth five or six times a day. I made an effort to learn the pace and routine of her life so that I could call her when she was most likely to be alone, and to my great pleasure I realized that she was making the same sorts of calculations about me. Her husband knew nothing about any of this, nor did my girlfriend. We conducted our relationship as though it was an affair, except for one thing: it was not an affair. It seemed better—or safer, at least—to spend hours a day fantasizing about her than to face the consequences of a real relationship. Perhaps I sensed that a short-term fling would be impossible, that once it began there would be no going back.

The prospect of hurting my girlfriend and destroying Jane's marriage tormented me, as did the fear that, having robbed her of her past, I might not be able to give her a future.

Jane had a simpler take on things: she thought we should sleep together. She announced this matter-of-factly at one of our lunches, adding that her husband would be leaving on a week-long golf vacation that very evening. This happened four days before I found Kirby Jussel on that roadside, and I had neither heard from her nor attempted to contact her since she folded her key into my hand and brushed her lips against my cheek, light as vapor.

Perhaps, in some strange way, my failure to show up at Jane's house was what prompted me to drive back to Roy Jussel's place that morning, the sun drowning in a thick dawn fog. I can't describe how I found my way through that haze to the rusted mailbox with his name on it; all I remember is feeling the need to act.

* * *

Jussel was already loading a shovel into his pickup truck as I arrived. He seemed surprised to find me in his driveway, but no more surprised than I was to be there.

"I was hoping to come with you," I stammered.

He stared at me, expressionless, and for a moment I feared he was going to hit me with the shovel.

"Now, why would you want to do that?" he said.

"I don't know. I'm still in town. I'm awake. I thought you might need some help."

He thought about it for what seemed like a long time, and then he shrugged and gestured to another shovel leaning against the side of the house.

"Shit, why not? The digging will go faster with two."

"I hope you don't mind me asking this," I said, grabbing the spade and tossing it into the truck. "But what, exactly, are we digging for?"

He held up his left hand, the one that had been wrapped in his security blanket the day before. Even in the thin dawn light, I could see that it was strangely jaundiced and stiff. Then, with a quick motion, he grabbed that hand with his other one and pulled on it sharply. A prosthetic limb popped off, and Roy Jussel held out the stump of his left arm, cleanly severed a few inches above the wrist.

★★★

The truck's suspension was shot and the roads to the lake were unpaved. I remember that trip as if it were some surreal amusement park ride—me trying to stave off nausea (whether from carsickness, the image of his mutilated arm, or simple dread, I'll never be sure) while Roy sat calmly at the wheel, a cigarette perched between two of his imitation fingers, as he unfolded his story of betrayal and retribution.

"I had tried to stay away from Emily, tried to do right by my brother. Then one day he asked me to give her a ride home from his place. She never went back. I was in single-A ball that summer, pitching for the Hickory Crawdads, so she came out to live with me in North Carolina. When she first left him, Kirby had made a lot of threats—against her, against me, against himself—but we hadn't heard from him in months, and she was beginning to hope he'd moved on with his life. I knew better. My brother had never been one to turn the other cheek. Sure enough, one night he broke into our apartment."

Because the Jussel boys had shared a bed all those years, Kirby knew everything about the way his brother slept. He did not need a flashlight to find Roy in that room, lying on his stomach, his arm dangling off the side of the bed. Just by listening to Roy breathe, he could tell when his sleep was at its deepest. Kirby knew the way Emily slept, too, how she awoke at the slightest sound, so he had to be quick and careful, taking Roy's arm, putting it on the night stand, then lifting that axe above his head in the dark.

"I don't think he wanted to kill me, just make me hurt as bad as I'd hurt him. But I doubt I'd be talking to you now if not for Emily. One second, she was sound asleep; the next, she was leaping out of bed, tugging a belt from the blue jeans I'd worn that night, and lashing it around my arm for a tourniquet. Kirby, he looked like a madman when the lights came on, but as he stumbled out of there he was holding my hand palm-in-palm, the way he did when I was a little boy and still attached to it. Afterward, he sent me pictures—on one of them, no lie, he was pretending to fondle himself with my fingers—but I never went to the police. I told everyone around here I'd been in a bad car wreck out east; if they didn't believe me, that was their problem. Emily, as you can imagine, was real freaked out, and I couldn't blame her for opening up to a few people. But whenever stories started floating around this town, I would deny them. I couldn't forgive my brother, but locking him up wouldn't have fixed anything. So we shared the secret, but it was the last thing we shared. We never spoke again."

When we arrived, the sun was beginning to burn through the mist on Demerest Lake. We took out our shovels and began to dig. It did not take long. About twelve feet from the willow tree that Kirby had described, my spade hit something hollow sounding, buried about eighteen inches deep. It was a five-gallon pickle drum made of green plastic and bearing the logo of a fast-food chain. Roy peeled the lid up, peered inside, then sealed it again. The smell of formaldehyde lingered in my nose for a long while afterward.

"What are you going to do with it?" I asked him as we loaded it into the truck.

"I suppose I'll figure out a way to bury it with Kirby," he said. "It meant more to him than to me anyway."

"So it doesn't bother you at all—I mean, losing your baseball career and all that?"

"Hell, yes, it bothers me," he said. "I've got nothing but regrets. But I wouldn't change a thing if it meant I had to give up Emily. Not if I could reattach my hand, not even if I could bring my brother back to life."

We drove back to his place, then he invited me inside for a beer. Neither of us had much to say. As I left that day, another car was pulling into the driveway. I was surprised to discover that she was no great beauty, just a tired-looking woman on the verge of middle age.

***

My wife can be a difficult person. She is strongly opinionated but tends to change those opinions on a whim, so that what made her furious one week can make her ecstatic the next. Her frankness sometimes alienates her from people, including my own parents. She has a lovely singing voice but an intolerance for those who do not have the same ear or training; when I try to play Bob Dylan in the car, she will often sing over his songs, on key, like a schoolmarm sternly correcting an inept and intransigent pupil. (I know it's petty of me to mention this, but still.) She remains sensitive about her inability to bear children but, to my delight, has finally agreed to consider adoption. We still live in Indiana, but I do not travel anymore. I found that I could not bear to be away from her.

I don't talk much about the Jussel boys. My wife, who tries to change the subject whenever it comes up in public, calls the tale "morbid," though part of her discomfort, I suspect, is that her own role in it is so small. The version of events she tells, which begins roughly where this one leaves off, is a more traditional love story about a man who saved a woman from an unhappy marriage and a woman who saved a man from himself. All true, and yet none of it would have happened if I had not stolen Roy Jussel's security blanket that day.

I had just finished my last lukewarm sips of beer and was about to thank my host and depart when the phone rang. Roy had been rushing to the kitchen all morning to answer condolence calls, some of them, no doubt, from the very same people who had spoken so unkindly of him the night before. These conversations clearly made him uncomfortable, and he politely but firmly cut each one off after a few perfunctory words. This call, however, turned out to be from the undertaker, and as their discussion bogged down in the details of the coffin and headstone and wake and funeral, it occurred to me that I now had several minutes alone to explore Jussel's house. The place had seemed overfilled and chaotic when I came in, but now, as I paced the living room, I began to perceive a strange beauty. The walls, decorated with dozens of children's drawings, were cracked and warped and dented, but the yellow paint was so fresh it still smelled. The furniture was old and worn, but everything seemed right where it should be: in an elegant leaded-glass bookshelf, missing several panes, I noticed a collection of flint arrowheads on one shelf, and, on the next, *The Collected Stories of Eudora Welty,* a Bible, and a thumb-worn copy of Flannery O'Connor's *A Good Man is Hard to*

Find. A few snapshots of children hung above the mantelpiece, but otherwise the walls were surprisingly free of photos. This was not the kind of house, I realized, which needed portraits to prove that it was occupied by a close-knit family. Down the hallway, a door opened into a darkened bedroom. Folded neatly on one of the pillows was a frayed piece of satin. I lifted it to the side of my face: it felt like a kiss.

I would have written Roy Jussel long ago if I could find the words. I would have explained that it was nothing personal, that sometimes you hurt others without wanting or meaning to—but he knows all about that. I would have told him I regret what I did, only it isn't true. I would have let him know why I stole it if I were sure myself. I would have sent the blanket back, but my gut tells me I relieved him of a great burden. (Jane didn't want it around the house, but I couldn't bring myself to throw it out. In the end, I left it in a Salvation Army drop box.) Yet none of that was on my mind as I sped away from his house, the blanket wrapped around my neck, full of his scent. Nor was I thinking of Jane, though I would wind up at her door that night, fidgeting with a key. My thoughts were lost in a flurry of black wings, the birds flashing like shards of a midnight sky as they swarmed down from the tree and strutted over the corpse, oblivious to their own beauty or the dead man's sorrows, conscious only of the banquet ahead.

THE MASTER OF PATINA

Part One: Clio

In the summer, children of our city began to find coins among the cobblestones. The first of these were bronze, with delicate patinas outlining profiles of emperors wearing laurels or crowns or turbans and empresses with spirals of plaited hair twisting on top of their heads into the shapes of serpents or birds. Scholars could not identify these rulers, nor could they interpret the images on the reverse sides—a cracked goblet, a prone acrobat whose legs looped back around to rest on his head, a jaguar with seven eyes, a map of a land unknown. The detail was stunning. Examined under a microscope, one piece was found to contain an ornate staircase in the shape of a double helix, on which tiny figures were descending endlessly into the center of the coin; another depicted a window opening into a second window, inside of which stood a beautiful long-necked woman. More coins started to appear, these of silver and gold. Philologists declared the legends indecipherable, a runic language forgotten to time. A few stubborn skeptics questioned the artifacts' authenticity, asking how it could be possible that they would simply appear along the boulevards, as if dropped from heaven. But for the rest of us—we who took to the streets on our hands and knees, oblivious to horse droppings from the milk carts and butchers' wagons, oblivious to motorcar traffic, which we brought to a standstill all over town, oblivious to our filthy clothes and bloodied knees and sometimes to our spouses, children, and jobs—those coins were evidence of a lost civilization far superior to our own.

Then one day, the manna was gone. We turned up rings, keys, buttons, spoons, strands of silver twine, the broken blade of a pocket knife, a tarnished bracelet bearing the name of a man none of us could recall. A certain stevedore, looking in an alley near the docks, discovered his own glass eye, which had popped out in a fistfight the previous year. But he alone could count himself lucky; the rest of us continued to come up empty-handed. Undaunted, we rose early each morning to comb through the lanes, our numbers continuing to grow until the day a rumor began to circulate through our ranks. Police, it was said, had picked up a young artist and charged him with forgery. Not only had he manufactured the coins but also a series of sculptures previously thought to be of great antiquity, two of which stood at the entrance to our National Museum of Art.

★★★

From the beginning, he was all we ever talked about. Rightists claimed he was an anarchist, attempting to foment chaos and topple ruling institutions. Leftists insisted he was a government agent, spreading counterfeit specie in order to distract the proletariat from society's injustices. Spiritualists of various sects hailed him as a time traveler, a wizard, a visitor from Mars. But we who thronged the granite courthouse steps for the trial's opening session found the defendant to be disappointingly average looking. Solid if not quite stocky, he was physically unremarkable except for a thick shock of silver hair, which "instead of making him look older than his thirty-six years, gave that genius of deceit an air of agelessness," wrote one of the many reporters covering what the newspapers, poking fun at the epic scope of the alleged hoax, had dubbed "The Trial of the Centuries." Surrounded by a phalanx of constables, the prisoner pushed through the crowd with a blank expression, followed by a girl, perhaps twelve years of age, with wild hair and a frayed gingham dress—his daughter, it was whispered, though many of us mistook her for some street waif who had fallen in at his heels.

The people of our country had once worshipped youth and dreamed the honeyed dream of eternal progress. Who among us can say why or even when our faith began to wane? Failed wars, economic disasters, political upheavals, natural catastrophes—worn down by such traumas, we grew fatalistic, eventually accepting as incontrovertible the notion that nothing was possible in our own time, that history had run its course, that everything of beauty or value belonged to the past. At first we focused our backward gaze on the generation just before us, praising our parents' era as the height of tranquility and prosperity, but soon we began to search for a golden age in the deeper recesses of time. Nostalgia became the de facto state religion, relics the national obsession. The poor dug up their yards in search of arrowheads, rusty nails, marbles, medicine bottles. The rich bought statues of gods.

When those coins began to appear on our streets, we saw them as final proof of a bygone age somehow more authentic than our own. Not even the arrest could shake our faith. How was it possible, we asked, for a lone man to conceive of, design, and manufacture so many tiny artifacts, much less finance the whole undertaking? The raw metals alone, we pointed out, were worth a fortune. What could motivate someone to toss silver and gold into the streets? That question seemed to stump even prosecutors, who made no reference to the coins in their indictment. The evidence, they insisted, showed beyond a shadow of a doubt that the accused had, in fact, minted the mysterious coins. But because he did not profit from them, no law had been broken. The case against the counterfeiter would have to hinge on the statues, which had sold for untold millions.

***

The prosecution's star witness was an elderly man who radiated a sense of old-fashioned grace, his bald head bearing the same stately luster as the courtroom's polished oak walls. Although the newspapers reported he was a coconspirator who had only agreed to testify after a promise of immunity, he did not seem the least bit uncomfortable on the stand. Slipping a well-manicured hand onto our holy book and swearing to tell the unvarnished truth, he flashed a smile as dapper and sleek as his hand-tailored silk suit.

"Please tell the court your line of work, sir," began the prosecutor, a plump man with curly red muttonchops like animal pelts.

"I am a dealer of fine art."

"You specialize in pieces of considerable antiquity, do you not?"

"That is correct."

"But in this case, they only *appeared* to be antique, am I right?"

"Much to my shame, yes."

"As a matter of fact, I'd like you to identify one of those items now," said the prosecutor, nodding to a pair of bailiffs at the rear of the room. The huge doors swung open, and the sound of screeching wheels echoed in from the corridor. Four more bailiffs appeared, pushing a hand truck that bore a large wooden crate. With great effort, and a few curses (at which we could not contain our laughter), they guided it up the aisle, brought it to a stop near the bench, and began to unhook the panels.

Inside stood a life-sized bronze of a beautiful long-necked woman with drowsy eyes, a high-girdled tunic clinging tightly to the contours of her figure. Her thick hair flying behind her, as if whipped by the wind, she rode a chariot conveyed by neither horses nor wheels but by eagle wings sprouting from the vehicle's sides. In her right hand, she held a reed pen, and in her left a scroll, its long papyrus wrapping around her hip before flying off the rear of the chariot. A blue-green patina shrouded her whole form, making her appear somehow distant, even ghostlike, as if we were seeing her through a thick fog.

"Do you recognize this work?" asked the prosecutor.

"I'm afraid so," replied the witness with a resigned smile.

"Would you be so good as to describe it to the court?"

"Well, certainly. This statue—or, as I must teach myself to say, this *forgery*—depicts Clio, muse of history. Her winged chariot is meant to represent the rush of time. She is recording events as they occur, and, as you can see, the papyrus flutters away so as to suggest her work is infinite—not unlike that of the lovely lady to my right."

The court reporter, a prim, chinless woman, looked up from her stenograph machine with a blush. We saw it and chuckled, not wanting to like this man, not wanting to believe him, but feeling charmed nonetheless. The judge banged his gavel.

"And this forgery—you sold it through your gallery, correct?" asked the prosecutor.

"Unwittingly, but yes," said the witness. He then identified the buyer—the chairman of a streetcar company—and named the price, which caused a collective gasp.

"And where did you get it?"

"From a scam artist—a man who deceived me and ruined my good name."

"Would you be so kind as to point this person out to the court?"

"Certainly," said the old man, pointing. "That's him. That's the charlatan."

We all turned to the defendant, anxious to find out how he would respond. But it was his daughter, seated behind him, who rose to her feet.

"No," she told the old man, her stare fierce, her voice barely more than a whisper. "It was the other way around. You came to him. You took advantage."

The judge slammed his gavel. "Sit, young lady," he said. "Restrain yourself."

She did not move, her gaze still locked on the witness, who flashed an unperturbed grin but (we saw) averted his eyes. "My mother was dying," she said, her words growing both softer and more assertive. "We needed money for medicine. You took advantage."

The gavel fell five more times before the judge could restore order, after which he warned the girl he would not tolerate another outburst and lectured the rest of us about decorum. Through it all, the defendant never looked up. We later heard from those in the front row that he sketched a woman's torso over and over in his notebook—shoulders, clavicle, breasts, stomach, hips, shoulders, clavicle, breasts, stomach, hips, always the same.

***

Persephone, queen of the underworld, perched on her throne; Isis, goddess of ten thousand names, nursing her child; Hera, queen of Mount Olympus, pomegranate in hand; Diana the huntress, arrow drawn—by the end of the art dealer's three days of testimony, these bronze nudes stood side by side, each one more beautiful than the last, all of them with long necks and drowsy eyes. And though we who were there on that day have now grown old, we can picture those statues still, nebulous and evanescent, more like longings than memories. We will carry those images to our graves—a sandaled foot, an outstretched hand, the precise bend of an earlobe, everything awash in green.

The longer we stared at them, the less it seemed to us that the silver-haired man was on trial but the statues themselves. We waited anxiously for someone to speak on their behalf, to assure us that they had come from a world distant from our own and more enlightened. And so, when the old man finally finished his testimony and the defense attorneys announced they would not cross-examine, we were stunned. A silence fell over the hall. Beneath the weight of those sculptures, the floorboards seemed to moan.

The prosecution's next witness was a constable from the graveyard shift, who described how, while making the rounds late one starless night, he had watched from the shadows as a girl in a hooded shawl dropped a glimmering object to the cobblestones near the hippodrome. Discovering that it was a coin—a silver piece with a man holding a dead swan, its neck limp in his fist, on one side, and a windowless tabernacle on the other—he decided to follow her at a safe distance. Wandering a maze of darkened lanes, changing directions every few blocks and stopping three times to drop more coins, the girl led him at last to the old meatpacking district, a squalid area in which artists and other bohemian squatters had set up makeshift homes in abandoned slaughterhouses that still bore the faint smell of rot and blood. At the doorway to one such building, where a lamp glowed through a dirty first-floor window, she stopped, glanced over her shoulder, and, still not noticing her pursuer, who crouched in an alley, pushed inside. He raced after her, pounded on the door, and, when no one answered, took a step back and kicked it down.

"And whom did you discover?" asked the prosecutor.

"That girl," said the constable, pointing to the defendant's daughter. "And *him*."

"What else did you see?"

"Coins, ancient-looking, all spread out nice and neat on a big table."

"Was that all?"

"On the second floor, he had a studio. There was a foundry up there for smelting metals. There were lots of chemicals, blow torches, that sort of thing. And there were molds all over the place—small ones for the coins and big ones for the statues."

"The statues you see before you now?"

"I couldn't say, sir. The molds weren't of whole bodies, just parts—an arm here, a leg there, a head across the way. All of them belonged to women—the *same* woman, if the girl is to be believed. She said her late mother had been the model for every last one."

* * *

The defense attorneys did not cross-examine the constable, nor did they choose to interrogate any of the other prosecution witnesses: a precious-metals wholesaler who identified receipts and purchase orders, signed by the artist, for silver and gold as well as for the copper and tin used to make bronze; a scientist who testified the metals in the statues were chemically identical to samples found in the studio; and a professor of art who matched the molds to the sculptures and showed how the various parts all fit together.

By the time the prosecution rested, doubt was beginning to thicken in our bones. When we stared at the statues, we still felt certain they came from dirt-floored workshops, dense with the smell of molten metal and lit only by charcoal furnaces, where forgotten artisans pumped bellows and poured red-hot ore into molds, their eyes aglow with divine inspiration. Yet when we turned away, the spell was broken, the logic of the prosecution's case inescapable, the voices in our heads whispering that those sculptures were just meaningless fabrications of a cynical confidence artist. Anguished, we held out hope the accused would make sense of it all when he came to testify. He never took the stand.

The defense called just a single witness—one of the purported victims, the chief curator of the National Museum of Art. Before the questioning began, bailiffs wheeled in two more statues, which, when finally hoisted into place, towered over the heads of the others. These nudes were nearly identical—one of them holding aloft an oil lamp, the other a chalice. They appeared at once monumental and tenuous, their emerald patinas so ethereal that a greenish hue seemed to seep into the air, surrounding the statues with a mothball light, almost liquid, as if those goddesses presided over some lost city submerged centuries ago to the ocean floor.

THE DEFENSE: You purchased these two statues for your institution, correct?

THE WITNESS: Yes, well, they were sort of a matched

set—Mnemosyne, the goddess of memory, and her sister, Lesmosyne, who presides over forgetting. That's her on the right, offering a drink of water from the River Lethe.

THE DEFENSE: And you must regret buying such forgeries.

THE WITNESS: Well, I suppose I would—if I considered them forgeries.

THE DEFENSE: Excuse me, sir. Did you hear the testimony of the previous witness? Did you see the exhibits presented by the prosecution?

THE WITNESS: I'm aware of this evidence. But I'm also aware of other evidence—even more convincing evidence, I believe.

THE DEFENSE: And would you describe this evidence to the court?

THE WITNESS: Certainly. The museum recently commissioned an independent panel of top experts from all over the country to do thorough scientific testing on these items.

THE DEFENSE: And what did those experts determine?

THE WITNESS: That the statues are between 2,300 and 2,500 years old.

THE DEFENSE: Wait, sir. Are you actually suggesting that these works are authentic?

THE WITNESS: I'm suggesting that the distinction between authentic and counterfeit may be moot in this case. I'm suggesting that—and I can't explain this—the defendant has the power to bring the present into the past. I'm suggesting that he can make new things old.

For a brief moment, silence hung over the room like dust motes in the thick citrus sunlight that streamed in through high windows. And even then, before the gasps and shouts and laughter, before the hardwood echo of the gavel, before we rose and rushed to the defendant, shoving aside his daughter as we tried to touch his threadbare suit—even then, we had already convinced ourselves that we were saved from oblivion.

Oh, to live those few seconds again! To feel that history had embraced us. To believe that like those statues, we would endure forever, not wither away as we have, the years rushing past, everything blurring and fading, everything drifting into dreams, our story coming to an end with the four most ruinous words ever spoken: *once upon a time.*

Part Two: Hebe

The prisoner worked in the mailroom, which gave him the opportunity to smuggle in all kinds of contraband—rum, opium, brass knuckles, knives. These items were as useful to him inside the penitentiary as those bronze nudes had been in his days as a respected broker of fine art. Although he now wore prison stripes instead of hand-tailored silk suits, he remained, even with rheumatism and failing vision, a consummate dealmaker. Inmates joked that for the right price he could sneak a whole herd of elephants inside those walls, a naked beauty queen riding bareback on every last one. It became customary that men going up for parole would touch his bald head for good luck—a privilege for which he always charged.

The Trial of the Centuries had ended with a stunning reversal of fortune—the defendant cleared on all counts, his chief accuser charged with perjury. Sentenced to ten years, the old man now found himself in the ancient limestone fortress that housed the country's worst criminals. He had always dreaded this fate, but once inside, he came to see prison as a kind of retirement home, and a pleasant one at that, a place that not only took care of all his physical needs but also returned him to a position of prestige and power. It did not grieve him to think he might never see the outside world again. He knew that he would not be welcome back in polite society and that if he happened to outlive his jail term he would be forced to scratch out an income by swindling elderly ladies out of their pensions, just as he had done at the start of his career. Rather than stooping to such petty scams, he preferred to die in the reformatory, unreformed, unbowed, unrepentant about anything he had done or anyone he had harmed. He had just one worry, a doubt that plagued him only in the dark, only in the dead of night when he awoke to a whisper.

"Did you see her? Did you ever actually see her?"

Sometimes he thought the words came from one of the inmates in adjacent cells, and other times he decided they weren't words at all but the skittering of skeletal prison rats or a chorus of frogs from some pond beyond the walls. But even if the question had emerged from the murky depths of some dream, he felt compelled to sit up and reply.

"Don't be stupid," he would hiss. "I know her body better than those of all the society ladies who sent their maids home early and waited for me behind lace curtains, better than those of their pretty daughters who let me rob them of their innocence like we were playing three-card Monte, better than those of all the women who trembled beneath me in penthouses and flophouses and whorehouses, in haylofts and alfalfa fields and dark corners of train stations and alleys stinking of piss. I know the precise angle of that little scar on her left eyebrow, the exact position of that mole in the small of her back."

"Because you cast her sculptures in bronze—or because you saw her in the flesh?"

The more he contemplated the question, the less he was sure of an answer. In the dark, he would remember how he had first stumbled upon those beautiful clay nudes, every one of them in her image, at some back-alley gallery with cracked walls and grimy windows; how he showed up at the sculptor's studio the next day, deciding to come right out and confide to the artist that he made his living by passing off modern bronzes as the work of ancients, that he could no longer keep up with demand, and that he had decided to hire an apprentice; how he assured the young man that the pay would be generous (more in a year than the sculptor could hope to make from his own work in a decade) and that the only requirement would be to produce a few statues that looked enough like antiquities to deceive gullible collectors; how his host strolled silently to the door and signaled for him to leave; how he returned the next day and the day after that, showing up punctually every morning for weeks, only to be turned away each time. And if he could not now recall seeing her on any of those occasions, he felt somehow sure she had been there nonetheless, listening to everything, watching from the shadows.

He remembered the day he rushed back to the studio, having heard a rumor that the woman was in the hospital, seriously ill, her own doctors unable to do anything for her. She would require tests, costly medicines, perhaps visits to specialists abroad, the story went, but he did not let himself believe it until the artist swung open the door and ushered him inside, past a wild-haired girl who was skipping rope across the concrete floor, and into a stuffy, windowless back room. There, the sculptor made two demands. First, he would be a full and equal partner in the counterfeiting enterprise, not a mere apprentice. Second, the old man must teach him everything he knew about the craft.

Though hardly a man of honor, the forger had made sure to keep his side of the bargain, introducing his new protégé to the ancient art of lost-wax casting—making a ceramic mold of an original clay sculpture, preparing and pouring the molten metal (while taking care that the alloy contained no zinc, a dead giveaway for a modern forgery), breaking the mold from the freshly hardened bronze with hammers and chisels, grinding away mold marks and other imperfections, soldering the various sections together, and buffing out the finished sculpture. "But by far the most important part of this process," the old man had once explained, "is the patina. That, my friend, is where we make our money. Instant antiquity, I call it. Mix a few chemicals together, cause a bit of colored corrosion, and— presto!—before your eyes an object transforms into something timeworn, worthy of respect, and, if you are like the majority of our credulous countrymen, *genuine.*"

But who was the fool now? Who could no longer tell true from false? Sometimes the prisoner thought he was going senile. Sometimes the past seemed as opaque as one of those exquisite patinas the young artist had taught himself to make, mastering the old man's favorite formula (one part ammonium chloride, three parts cream of tartar, three parts sodium chloride, dissolved into twelve parts boiling water and mixed with twelve parts copper nitrate solution), before experimenting with other recipes, adding a bit of one chemical, subtracting a bit of another until he learned to change the color of bronze from light green to jade to malachite to olive. After many long nights spent tinkering with application methods—dabbing compounds onto the metal with a cloth or painting them on with a bristle brush or firing them with a huge blow torch—he knew at last how to create just the right hue for Aphrodite emerging from the bath or for Ma'at striding forward, scepter in one hand, ankh in the other, ostrich feather adorning her head.

But technical skill was only part of his gift. From the start, the old man felt his protégé had an uncanny effect on those bronzes, giving them not just tints of green and blue but something ineffable, something that could not be created by chemicals alone. There were moments, in fact, when he began to forget they were forgeries, began to believe the lies he kept telling clients who bid feverishly against each other to buy the works, began to let himself imagine sweat-soaked men in pith helmets unearthing the sublime sculptures from some dusty dig site. Even now, even in this cell, he would still catch himself thinking of the woman as somehow transcendent—not a goddess (he was too unsentimental to see any member of her sex in such terms) but more like a muse, a guiding spirit, a female figure for whom, unlike the drunk mother who had abandoned him when he was six or the silent aunt who had raised him with stern indifference, he could feel something other than contempt. He pictured the way she would sigh through the side of her mouth as she held a pose on the modeling stand, the way a distracted smile would curl across her lips, the way she would wink at him from across the studio. And yet he could never quite remember an instance in which any of this had actually happened.

"Did you love her?"

"*Love* her? Does a flesh peddler love his whore? I sold her body for millions. She made me rich. That's as close as I come to love."

It was true that the prisoner had never viewed human relationships as anything but a means of satisfying his ambitions and desires. He was neither ashamed nor proud of this; he simply accepted it as a central fact of his personality, the thing that made him so good at confidence tricks and other seductions. But when he thought of her now, he could sometimes feel clay caked to his fingers and palms, his own hands caressing an unfinished statue of her beautiful body. Then he had to remind himself that another man had made those statues, that what he remembered could never have taken place, that the sense of wonder he felt when he thought of that woman must be simple physical arousal.

Of one thing he was certain, however. He had once heard her voice. It happened after she came home from the last of many hospital visits, her case hopeless, a rare cancer overtaking her body. For thirteen days the old man went to the studio, and for thirteen days no one answered. On the fourteenth, his ear pressed to the door, he made out the murmur of the sculptor and the faint whisper of a woman. *Is it done, my love?* he thought he heard her say. On the fifteenth, the door swung open, and the artist stood alone, his clothes disheveled, his silver hair unwashed, his green eyes bloodshot. Glancing around, the old man found the place in disarray—half-eaten meals rotting on chipped plates and roaches skittering across the littered floor. In the center of this mess stood a new work in clay, a life-sized female figure with arms extended, her upturned palms holding aloft a large dish.

The counterfeiter had instantly identified the subject of that sculpture—Hebe, goddess of youth, offering the occupants of Mount Olympus a bowl of ambrosia, the food that gave them ageless immortality. But the figure itself shocked him. The face was hollowed into a skeletal grimace, the once-graceful neck now a shriveled tangle of muscles and tendons, the eyes almost shut. The spinal bones protruded like geological outcroppings, as did the ribs. The shrunken breasts hung slack. Surgical scars, half-healed and swollen, zigzagged across the loose flesh of the abdomen. The arms, thin and brittle as old bamboo, looked as though they might break under the weight of that bowl.

For once, the old falsifier found himself at a loss for words. Out of habit, he scanned the room a final time but knew now that the woman was gone and would not be coming back. And he knew as well that his partnership with the artist was at an end.

"I can't sell this piece," he said. "Not even an idiot would mistake it for real."

"I don't want you to sell it," replied the other. "I want you to help me cast it."

A small funeral took place the next week. The old man was not invited, but curiosity soon impelled him on a pilgrimage to her grave marker—a polished bronze statue of Hebe, goddess of youth. The artist, he observed, had chosen to forgo a chemically created verdigris, opting instead for what the ancients called *aerugo nobilis,* or noble patina, which no amount of human ingenuity can produce, only the passage of time.

On the following month, coins began to appear among the cobblestones.

Near the end of his life, his memory and eyesight both growing dim, the prisoner returned again and again to a vision that had come to him in the courtroom. He had forgotten it for years, but now it seemed stunningly vivid. The chief curator of the National Museum of Art was just finishing his testimony, the people leaping from their seats and rushing to the artist, the amber sunlight streaming in from high windows. As the old man watched from the rear of the gallery, someone in the front row glanced at him over her shoulder, a long-necked woman with drowsy eyes. And then she turned back, and the mob pushed past her. He rose from his seat and tried to make his way forward, but it was no use. Where the woman had stood, he saw only the thin shoulders of that girl with wild hair.

No one knew better than he that a lie told often enough takes on the shape and sheen of truth, that memory is the ultimate counterfeiter. It did not escape him that the last fraud he would ever commit might be on himself.

"Did you see her?"

"I'm absolutely sure of it," he whispered. Then he lay back in bed, confident at last that no voices would ever rouse him again.

Part Three: Mnemosyne and Lesmosyne

The man with silver hair was reading at his desk when the girl entered the room. She did not say a word, and if not for the slight swish of her dress and the ticking of a pendant watch around her neck, he might not have been aware of her at all. He did not look up. He knew that she wanted something from him, but he also knew that she was supremely patient and deferential to his whims. He had grown accustomed to making her wait.

The book was an insect encyclopedia, now illuminated by a kerosene lamp that cast its wavering glow across a lithograph of a tiny, almost translucent creature labeled "worker termite." *Despite being blind, these pests can devour an entire house in about two years,* the book said, *a feast consisting of millions of infinitesimal bites.* The artist lingered on that idea, pondering the ways he might put these insatiable insects to work.

When he first started making those coins, he had not yet fully formulated the idea of turning back the clock one object at a time. Everything he did was driven by grief. Inducing nicks and scratches in a piece of furniture, creating spiderweb imperfections in the glaze of a ceramic, applying gentle wear patterns to the edge of a plate, mastering varnish and heat to produce fine cracks on a painting's surface, causing marble to age with a simple solution of potato mold, sending his daughter on secret missions in the middle of the night, her pockets jingling—these were ways he mourned his wife.

He did not weep. He did not attempt to console the child. Words had never come easily to him, and what could he have said to her that would bring either of them any comfort? At the wake, he surprised himself by flying into a rage when elderly relatives told him how the girl was starting to look just like her mother. After a few drinks, he grabbed the child's wrist and, as bewildered mourners stood by, catalogued the differences—her nose was too big, her hair too curly, her eyes the wrong shade of blue. She did not protest, just stared at him with an expression of numb despair—the same look she wore a few weeks later when the constable led her father away to jail. He left her trembling in the doorway, a tiny figure silhouetted by lamplight. He could barely bring himself to turn around then—and in the five intervening years, not looking at her had become a habit.

The girl now let out something resembling a sigh, which he barely heard beneath an oddly poetic word for termite echoing inside his head. *Because it feeds on dead plant material such as wood, bark, and straw, returning nutrients to the soil through its feces and saliva, the termite is a highly efficient decomposer.* Decomposer—a blighter of composition. And wasn't that his own calling now? Human termite. Anticreator. Unmaker.

He had once thought it was the other way around—that composition could bring her back. In jail, he spent entire days sketching her hands, nose, eyes, trying not to forget the tiniest detail. He had been drawing her for so long that even before her death she sometimes seemed more real on paper than in person. It had been that way ever since the first time she slipped out of a robe in that life-drawing course at the Academy of Fine Art all those years before. The professor, a corpulent man who smelled of onions and absinthe and turpentine, was notoriously strict—demanding that his students draw the same model for six hours each day and that the model hold the same pose every day for a week. Long before he spoke to her, the young man had explored and charted every muscle in his future wife's body, every inch of her skin. It was during those sessions that he made sudden, almost inexplicable progress as a draftsman, the professor shaking his head in confounded silence as he flipped through the sketches at the end of each day. Then the young man would take those drawings home and pin them up at his bedside, never sure, as he meditated over them by candlelight, whether he was more excited by the woman's flesh or his own skill. He fell in love with her through those pictures.

For weeks after she died, he had been able to resuscitate her in his sketchbook, but even before the trial came to an end, she was beginning to fade there too. Shoulders, clavicle, breasts, stomach, hips, shoulders, clavicle, breasts, stomach, hips—on the first day of testimony, he sketched her torso over and over, barely listening to the lies his former partner was telling while on the stand. But no matter how many drawings he made, some detail was always wrong, some part of her had vanished. And then, on that final day of the trial, an alarming thing happened. As he tried to sketch her, a small dark spot appeared in the center of the page and spread like spilled ink. He sat there, stunned, then grabbed a pair of thick spectacles that one his lawyers had left on the table, and leaned close. The fuzzy spores came into focus just as the smell filled his nostrils. Mold. Horrified, he tossed the sheet off—only to watch a new black flower bloom across the next page, obliterating everything.

* * *

Something resembling a sigh—then only the ticking of the pendant watch around her neck. It was not unusual for them to share long silences, father and daughter. On some days they went to the cemetery and sat for hours beneath the Goddess of Youth, never exchanging a word. Was he to blame if the girl was now a withdrawn seventeen-year-old with no close friends and little apparent interest in boys? If she felt lonely or angry or sad, she did not say so, and he did not ask. Nor did he inquire whether she resented him for not sending her to school, insisting she remain back at the studio to help him with his work.

He had never intended to drag her into this—but then again, he had never meant to become the leader of a cause. Those coins were a simple act of contrition, an anonymous apology to his countrymen for profiting from their collective sense of nostalgia and melancholy, which had engulfed him as well. It had begun as a kind of technical exercise, an attempt to test his skills as a miniaturist by reproducing an extremely rare gold coin commissioned in 1621 by King Sigismund III of Poland to celebrate the Catholic victory over the Ottoman Empire at the Battle of Chocim. After that, he began coming up with the designs himself, creating his own images, his own alphabets, his own numeration systems, his own increasingly complex set of symbols, which he learned to make smaller and smaller and smaller, until he could fit an entire universe on two sides of a single coin. He did not think the plan through, did not consider the possibility that he would be caught, much less that his trial would cause such an uproar. But after his acquittal, when fellow citizens hailed him as an alchemist, a shaman, a saint, he did not turn away. Their search for a lost past was now his own.

His first commission came from a wealthy couple who had recently built a mansion—one of those sprawling stone structures so popular among the rich in that aimless land, borrowing architectural features indiscriminately from various bygone eras. The task of patination was monumental, the work slow and exacting. He ordered his clients out of their home and sealed off the property, permitting entrance to no one but the girl and himself. In the conservatory, they threw away the priceless collection of orchids and began to grow weeds, brambles, and tropical vines, searching for the most robust and invasive specimens. In the library, they set up a makeshift lab, culturing mold samples in petri dishes atop the billiards table and testing them on the walls. They bred rats in the wine cellar and bribed the local dogcatcher to release unclaimed strays inside the gates, where the beasts soon began to wander in hungry, howling packs. It was later whispered that the artist and his little girl stole human corpses and left them in the bedrooms, perfuming the place with the smell of death. This was not true (they used pig cadavers), but only weeks after the owners finally returned to their decaying entrance hall and climbed the moss-covered marble staircase, they began to complain that the place was haunted, not by one but by hundreds of muttering ghosts. As word spread, so many curiosity seekers flocked to the estate that the occupants decided to find a more inhabitable house and turn this one into a museum. The place soon became a kind of shrine to all things lost and longed after. Many visitors swore they had caught faint glimpses of their own long-departed loved ones in those cold, shadowy corridors. But for the man they now called the Master of Patina, the past remained more elusive than ever.

Her voice thinning until it became the fog, everywhere and nowhere; her words vanishing syllable by syllable until he could not remember a single conversation; her presence fading until he was unable to recall the place she was born, the names of her parents, their faces, her handwriting, the books she read, the songs she played on that old piano in the studio, the things that made her laugh, the sound of her laughter, the words she murmured as she lay dying. He had begun to wonder whether he forgot it all or never quite noticed, whether the only part of her he had ever understood was her skin.

* * *

The ticking and its echo—and still he hesitated, and still he did not turn. Lately the girl had taken to wearing her mother's clothes (the white linen dress, the black silk faille skirt, the pendant watch of blue enamel, which had once hung around that lovely long neck), and there was something else strange about her appearance as well, something more pronounced with each passing day, something that made it even harder to glance up.

He wished he could look her in the eye. She was, he knew, a doting daughter and a brilliant young woman. Together, they had brought churches to gentle ruin. Together, they installed crumbling facades on banks, libraries, mansions of steel magnates, and city halls. Together, they transformed town squares into old-world markets, the smells of human waste, over-ripe bananas, roasted corn, and live poultry lingering in the air.

In recent years, she had begun to come up with technical innovations of her own, which, if not as audacious as his, were no less ingenious. He invented a huge coal-burning contraption to coat buildings with soot; she bred a hybrid species of moth that left clothes well-worn without eating holes in the fabric. One of her subtlest creations was a tiny attachment for motion-picture projectors, which, as the cone of light shot overhead and the piano began to play, gave audiences a sudden certainty that they were watching a movie beloved by generations before them. This comforted thousands in those days of desperate nostalgia—another example, he thought, of her quiet compassion.

She was working on a new project now, one that she had

kept from him, spending long nights alone in the privacy of her study. No doubt that was why she was here tonight. No doubt she wanted to tell him her plans, ask his advice. Slowly he closed the book, an unspoken invitation for the girl to speak. And still he hesitated, and still he did not turn.

* * *

His name. She did not say *father*. She whispered his name in a voice not her own, a voice no longer everywhere and nowhere but inches from his ear. He spun toward the sound. Staring back at him was a thirty-year-old woman with drowsy eyes—a flawless forgery.

"Why do you look away?" she said. "I thought this was what you wanted."

* * *

The tears on her cheeks, the confusion on her face, then horror, then hatred. The silent room, the white linen dress, the pendant watch of blue enamel, ticking, ticking.

* * *

And then she was forty and then she was seventy and then he watched her die. And he knew that instead of turning back the clock, he had only succeeded in speeding up time—streets crumbling beneath his feet and bridges rusting as he crossed them and weeds rushing on ahead of him as if to announce his arrival to future generations, which kept coming and going before his eyes, cities burning and great buildings tumbling to the ground, skyscrapers and factories and stadiums, even the art museum that had housed his bronzes for all those years, blocks of granite falling like hail, the statues of memory and forgetting buried under tons of rubble, crushed into a single, inextricable thing.

* * *

Once upon a time (for he had lost all track of it), a silver-haired man sat in a cemetery beneath a statue of a scarred goddess. A cold, colorless fog hung in the air, and, as a breeze rose, dead leaves swiveled from the trees. In the man's lap rested a large, disorderly stack of paper; in his hand was the stub of a charcoal pencil. He did not know how or why he came to be in this place, only that he was condemned to draw a female figure over and over, day in, day out. He was never sure about the identity of his subject—sometimes she seemed to be a beautiful woman and sometimes she seemed to be a sad young girl and sometimes she seemed to be the goddess herself—but he felt sure his curse would not be lifted until he captured her on the page, perfect in every detail. Only then would he find out who she was. Only then, when he recognized her for the first time, would he finally be released.

He closed his eyes and tried to picture her, the fallen leaves skittering past in waves. Sometimes, if he waited long enough, she would suddenly come close and stand just out of sight, a presence so real he could almost hear her through the mist, murmuring. *Is it done, my love?* she seemed to say. *Is our work complete at last?*

FOUR FACES

One: 2013

She once saw a woman shot to death at a nightclub. This was back in her early twenties, back when she was drunk all the time, back when she was still sleeping with men. The place was called the Phantom Limb, a dimly lit hipster dive in the Marigny district of New Orleans, the interior decor consisting of old prosthetic arms, legs, hands, and feet that dangled from the ceiling on wires. Sometimes, she'd just sit there, sipping vodka gimlets and watching artificial body parts vibrate in the rafters, a danse macabre set to the blare of indie rock. Other times, she'd try to make eye contact with women sitting at the opposite end of the bar, some fifty feet away. At that safe distance, she told herself, she could flirt without consequence. It was a game, a test run for something she wasn't quite sure she wanted. All her feelings seemed unreal in those days, emanating from something she couldn't see or touch, something no longer there, something similar to the name of that bar. Most women didn't even know she was staring at them, and those who happened to catch her gaze didn't hold it long, though a few seemed to offer a look of acknowledgement, or maybe even interest. What would she do if one headed her way for an actual conversation? So far, there'd been no need to figure it out. In her drunken haze, those far-off women seemed like hallucinations. Then one night she locked eyes with a fellow patron sitting all alone at the far end of the bar with a round face, a downturned mouth, and an expression that seemed sad and hopeful at the same time.

Somewhere in that crowded room, a disturbance erupted, men's angry voices rising over the music. Both women glanced at the fracas—somebody pushing somebody else in the darkness, somebody pushing back, then curses, shouts, threats, the usual stuff of a late Friday night—before they turned once more to each other. Silver-tinted pixie cut, earrings that looked like dangling silver coins, ice that shone silver in her highball glass, which she raised slowly to her lips and, without looking away, took a sip and smiled, an intimate smile, a conspiratorial smile, a lover's smile, a smile that lingered even after the burst of fire, bam, bam, bam, even after she started to fall.

That instant between the shooting and the falling would haunt the onlooker for years, that instant when life and death mingled on the woman's face. Still holding her highball glass, she did not look afraid or even surprised but exultant, expectant, ready to rise up, push through the crowd and introduce herself to the stranger across the bar.

Two: 2015

The number of an unknown caller from Florida appeared on her phone. Because she had recently joined Alcoholics Anonymous and was trying to live in the moment, trying to pay attention to the little things, she decided to answer. The woman on the other end had the calmest voice she'd ever heard, as silky and subtle and warming as vodka.

"Am I speaking with Deedra? Deedra Miller?"

The calmest voice she'd ever heard turned out to belong to an assistant coroner at the Treasure Coast County Medical Examiner's Office, who informed her that the body of a woman had washed up on a nearby beach. A tentative identification had been made, based on a driver's license found in the room of a guest who'd gone missing from a local hotel.

"We have reason to believe," said the woman, "that the decedent is your mother."

Three days later, after a plane trip from New Orleans to West Palm Beach with a three-hour layover in Atlanta, during which she broke down and had a couple drinks but still managed to make her connecting flight, Deedra was leaning over a gurney in the medical examiner's body-viewing room, staring into the wide-open eyes of a corpse.

"I can't be sure," she said. "Not a hundred percent, anyway."

"Take your time."

The voice came from behind her, the calmest one she'd ever heard. "Drowning victims," that voice softly intoned, "tend to have an otherworldly appearance."

The dead woman did indeed look like some alien from a science-fiction film, her face crimson and bloated and gelatinous. At first glance a few seconds earlier, Deedra had thought she might vomit all over the viewing room. But now the nausea had passed and something else was bothering her, something even more disorienting. She could pick out individual features of the person on the gurney—the familiar brown eyes, the wild tangle of curly hair, the birthmark below the right ear (a blemish which, if she looked in the mirror at this moment, she would see on her own neck). But the face as a whole belonged to a stranger, a person she'd walk right by if they passed on the street.

"Is it weird," Deedra said, "to recognize someone and yet not recognize her at all?"

"You're asking the wrong person," the assistant coroner replied with a languid chuckle. "I happen to have something called prosopagnosia—face blindness. To be honest, I'm lucky if I ever recognize anybody."

"Even people close to you?" Deedra inquired, studying the expressionless mouth of the corpse and wondering why she felt no emotion.

"I once took part in an autopsy for the victim of a car wreck. Removed and weighed her internal organs—heart, lungs, liver. Only later did I discover that she was one of my good friends. We'd met for coffee just a few days before the accident."

"How awful."

"The condition is hereditary, a gift from my mom," the assistant coroner said with another unhurried laugh. "But she gave me lots of good things as well."

"I haven't seen my mother in years," Deedra said, reaching out and touching the forehead of the corpse, its skin cool, chalky, a foreign substance.

"Perhaps she no longer matches your memory."

"No, she's unchanged. Frozen in time."

She wasn't making sense, even to herself. Feeling the need to explain—or perhaps to seek an explanation—she turned to the assistant coroner, a tall woman whose green eyes were as calm as her voice. Had she met this person somewhere before? The face was not animated or exotic, not even beautiful, really, or at least not in any identifiable way. Yet there was something about her, a presence that felt familiar—far more familiar, it now occurred to her, than that of the dead woman. And almost before she was aware of it, the words were flowing from her so effortlessly that it felt less like a story than a song, a breathless sea ballad about a little girl whose only sibling, a brother nine years older, disappeared without a trace one day while surfing, after which his mother came to hate the surviving child for living, for growing up, for not being frozen in time. And when the song drifted off, the assistant coroner was at her side, both of them peering into eyes stuck in the same gaze forever, eyes that looked through them, beyond them, as if staring up from the farthest depths of the ocean.

"My parents used to go to that beach every year," Deedra heard herself saying. "They'd bring home all these objects that happened to wash ashore, as if my brother was sending them some secret code—a house full of meaningless wreckage."

"It must have been a lonely place to grow up."

"Flotsam and jetsam," Deedra replied. "That's my brother and me—one of us accidentally washed into the sea, the other intentionally tossed overboard."

The assistant coroner studied the impassive face of the corpse. "One of the things we do around here," she said, "is determine the time of death. But it has always seemed to me that some people die long before their vital functions actually cease."

Then the tall woman reached over and squeezed Deedra's hand, a touch as satiny and reassuring as the first sip of a long-awaited drink, a touch that still lingered on her skin the following morning as she sat in a bar at West Palm Beach International Airport, waiting for a delayed flight and finishing off a vodka gimlet. On the TV behind the bar, there was a report on the local news about a man arrested for impersonating a priest, but she wasn't paying attention, wasn't thinking about anything but the unbeautiful face of a stranger who wouldn't even recognize her if they ever were to meet again. And later, after another flight delay and two more drinks, she realized she still had that stranger's work number on her phone. "Hello? Hello? Who is this?" the person on the other end kept saying, but the caller didn't respond, just closed her eyes, brought the tumbler to her lips, and listened one last time to the calmest voice she'd ever heard.

Three: 2016

Driftwood in all shapes and sizes, doll's heads, rubber duckies, a small wooden crucifix so seaworn the body of Jesus was smoothed down to a bump—everything into the fire. A thick plume of noxious-smelling smoke was rising over the neighborhood where she'd grown up in Kalamazoo, a black streak through the golden autumn sky. Sooner or later somebody would call the police, but for now she was on a roll. Lensless binoculars, long-empty miniature bottles of Dewar's, a coconut carved with menacing eyes and pointed teeth—more fuel for the burn barrel behind her parents' place, a house she hadn't visited since she left at nineteen, not even for her father's funeral the previous year or for her mother's burial a couple of months after that, when she'd missed the plane because she was wasted. A teardrop-shaped pointer from a Ouija board, a teak bookmark in the shape of a dagger, brittle old 78 rpm records bearing names of long-forgotten singers—Deedra hadn't had a drink in four months now, and before she flew out here to get the house ready for sale, her AA sponsor had warned that emotions can be overwhelming in early sobriety and that without the numbing effect of alcohol, recovering addicts often experience a powerful sense of anger. What he didn't say was how magnificent her rage would be, how exhilarating to feel like an exposed nerve, everything as bright and hot and intense as these cascading flames. Chess pieces from unmatched sets all over the world, the maple frame of a gearless, faceless cuckoo clock—she was practically sprinting now between house and blaze, determined to destroy everything, all that random refuse from other people's lives, other people's stories. How could her parents have ever imagined that such mismatched bits of beach trash would somehow form a story of their own, a series of clues would lead to their son? Flotsam and jetsam, brother and sister, husband and wife—a plastic wedding figurine joined the inferno, bride and groom instantly hissing into a molten lump. Flotsam and jetsam, flotsam and jetsam—hurling another armful into the blaze, she suddenly remembered one last object, a wooden barber shop pole she hadn't thought of in years, but now, coughing from the acrid smoke, she could picture it perfectly, the faded stripes, the wood as white and smooth as bone, the piteous look on her dad's face when she caught him hiding it from her mother, one more secret, one more silence, one more thing to rip out of that house and consign to the flames. Rushing inside, she searched everywhere, her brother's room, her parents' room, basement, attic, back to her brother's room, tearing open boxes, emptying drawers onto the floor, the pole nowhere to be found, but now she was in a frenzy, tipping over chairs and yanking framed photographs from the wall of the family room. Her brother on a bicycle before she was born, her brother in a Little League uniform, her brother and some girl she didn't recognize, dressed up for a high school dance—it thrilled her to smash the frames, pull the pictures out and watch the images ripple into ash, the lost boy finally disappearing from this house for good. Flotsam and jetsam, flotsam and jetsam, flotsam and jetsam—chanting the words between each breath, she dashed back inside for more pictures, shocked that so many contained her own face, as if she, too, had been missed, as if she, too, had been loved. A little girl on a teeter totter, a little girl curled up with a book, a little girl watching her big brother dangle a stick of marshmallows over this same burn barrel, his presence even then a shadow in the dusk—nothing spared from the blaze. Flotsam and jetsam—it was as if a melody were hidden beneath those words, something like a lullaby, the notes just out of reach. Flotsam and jetsam, flotsam and jetsam—more pictures into the inferno, most combusting instantly but one landing near the edge of the barrel. A little girl sucking her thumb, her chin resting on the shoulder of her mother, whose back was to the camera, holding her baby tight with both arms—Deedra stood there, waiting for the blaze to do its work and staring into the tired eyes of the girl, who suddenly seemed to be staring back. Something like a lullaby, the notes just out of reach—and before she knew it, she was thrusting her hand right into the flames, suddenly desperate to save that poor, lonely child.

Four: 2018

A classmate from her Nineteenth Century American Literature course caught up with her as she crossed the campus of the University of New Orleans one February afternoon. "I've been meaning to tell you something," he said. "There's a woman running around town who looks just like you—hundred percent identical. I keep spotting her from afar."

The young man flashed a knowing grin. She tried to remember his name. With his ironic clothes, air of studied slovenliness, and Abraham Lincoln beard, he reminded her of a tall, emaciated, unwashed leprechaun. In class, he always came in late and plopped down next to her, leaning over to whisper cryptic statements that seemed intended to arouse curiosity, make him seem mysterious and worldly. One thing she hadn't expected about going back to college at age twenty-seven was that she'd become an object of admiration.

"Are you making this up?" she asked.

"Swear to God, she could be your sister," he said, ambling off toward the cafeteria. "She's gorgeous. Maybe even as gorgeous as you. A drop-dead doppelganger."

They'd been using that word a lot in class. One of the previous week's assigned readings was Edgar Allan Poe's "William Wilson," a story about a drunken young man, estranged from his family and "addicted to the wildest caprices," who is shadowed by an alter ego—basically, a better version of himself. The climax comes at a masquerade ball during Carnival in Rome, where the two William Wilsons wind up in a fight to the death, though the story leaves it a mystery which one is murdered and which one survives.

Unlike most of her classmates, who either didn't bother to read the piece or saw it as "wordy and pretentious," as one of them put it, she couldn't get it out of her mind. Although she hadn't had a drink in close to two years, Deedra often felt that she, too, was locked in a life-and-death battle with another self, the winner still undetermined. Mardi Gras was now underway, a time that made her painfully aware of that previous Deedra, who often seemed more real and alive than the current, sober one. Although vaguely curious about her classmate's claim, she knew that this was no time for a recovering alcoholic to be wandering the streets in search of some random stranger to whom she bore a supposed resemblance. With the university beginning its spring break to coincide with the holiday, she resolved to lie low and catch up on homework.

She spent the first few days holed up in her Mid-City apartment, drinking Diet Dr. Pepper, watching competitive cooking shows on TV, searching the internet for good deals on vacation spots she never intended to visit, like Bali and Myanmar, and attempting to write a paper about the role of ambiguity in

Poe's short story "The Man of the Crowd." But late one afternoon, frustrated and bored, she decided to take her work to a
local coffee shop on Carrollton Avenue. Finding an open table
at the front window, she spread out her books, snapped open
her laptop, and tried to write but almost immediately found
it impossible. The laughter of fellow patrons, the clatter of
cups, the insistent, tobacco-smoke aroma of chicory-laced coffee, the half-eaten slice of avocado toast gathering dust under
a nearby table—all these distractions, which Deedra might not
have noticed on a normal day, now seemed to flood her senses
with a strange intensity, like light in dilated eyes. She contemplated leaving, but suddenly the dead air of her silent, spot-
less apartment seemed even more oppressive than the chaos
of this cafe. Ordering another cup of coffee, she opened *The
Complete Tales of Edgar Allan Poe* and began to skim through
"The Man of the Crowd" one more time, underlining passages
at random, but soon became absorbed in contemplation of the
scene outside.

Up until this hour, most of the passersby had worn street
clothes, walking their dogs or heading home from work or
scurrying from one appointment to another in their busy weekday schedules. But with the sun beginning to set, more and
more people were sauntering out in costume, their pace slower,
their bearing prouder, their gait more purposeful and expres-
sive. A woman in a zoot suit with eight-foot-long pants lurched
past on stilts, followed by a man in a monk's robe, a glow-in-
the-dark halo suspended impossibly over his bald scalp, which
he seemed to have shaved into a tonsure especially for the
occasion. Deedra had always loved the effort New Orleanians
expended on these extravagant, hand-crafted getups, all the
time and money and planning and passion they put into giving
themselves a new identity. Her old self had never felt more at

one with the city than at this time of year, when everyone was drunk and everyone was pretending to be someone else. Three years back, she'd gone as the "ghost writer," a costume she put together by purchasing a secondhand wedding dress and veil, slapping on some white face paint and blood-red lipstick, and walking around with a four-foot-long novelty pencil she'd picked up online. Such an odd alter ego, she now thought, for someone who never felt in control of events, someone who wasn't "authoring her own life," as they sometimes said in AA. But were things really that much better these days? Was she any more in charge, any closer to happiness? Gazing out the window at the growing procession of revelers, she consoled herself that—so far, at least—she'd managed to remain on this side of the glass. And then, on the opposite sidewalk, she spotted a woman of roughly her own height and carriage walking past in an oversized yellow sweater with a big zigzag black stripe—a sweater Deedra herself had knitted by hand.

Or at least it looked a lot like that sweater, a saggy, lopsided affair she'd undertaken as a means of occupying her mind during one of her many unsuccessful attempts to stop drinking. She'd originally intended it as a Christmas gift for her mother—yet another ill-conceived idea, another ornate exercise in self-hate, which she'd abandoned even before the ugly, ill-fitting item was finished. After wearing it around to the bars one night, during which time it managed to acquire a mysterious red stain (wine? pizza sauce? blood?), she'd banished it to a storage box in her closet. Or had she? Wasn't it at least possible that while on some spree she'd thrown it out or given it away or donated it to the Salvation Army? Her mind racing with all the improbable ways the sweater might have wound up with a stranger now disappearing down the street, Deedra rose and dashed out the door, not even bothering to collect her laptop or books.

"You," she shouted. "You in the yellow!"

The woman did not turn, but Deedra thought she recognized something familiar about her stride, something reminiscent of her own way of moving through the world, an aimless sway of the hips. She tried to remember if she'd glimpsed the woman's face.

"You!" she yelled again, but by now the woman was a full block ahead of her. As the distant silhouette disappeared around the corner, Deedra heard herself letting out a shriek, long and loud and shrill. She couldn't remember ever letting herself go like that, not even in her worst days of drinking, but she didn't stop until her lungs were drained.

The door of the coffee shop swung open, and her waiter emerged from inside, a pockmarked man wearing a greasy apron and a bemused smile.

"Excuse me, darling," he said, "but are you planning to pay?"

Humiliated, she dashed back inside, gathered her things, and, after shoving a wad of uncounted cash into the waiter's hands, rushed to her apartment in search of the sweater, which turned out to be right in the box where she'd remembered putting it—a discovery that filled her with both relief and disappointment. Unfolding the thing, she brought it to her nose and breathed in the unmistakably real smells of mothballs and wool, which seemed to offer some assurance that the last half hour's events had not been the product of some dream. Then she put the sweater away, returned the box to its proper place, made herself a cup of chamomile tea, opened the laptop, stared at the screen, snapped the computer shut again, and headed off in search of her doppelganger.

Yellow sweater, yellow sweater, yellow sweater, yellow sweater—stumbling around the city for days, she never saw anyone dressed that way again. But as Deedra wandered from place to place, Lakeview, City Park, Bayou St. John, Bywater, she kept having moments her Edgar Allan Poe-obsessed English professor might describe as uncanny, moments when she couldn't be sure whether she was the observer or the observed, the searcher or the one being sought. Was she imagining it, or did she keep spotting herself, always at a distance, always in a different guise? At the Krewe of Muses parade, there was a masked figure who blew Deedra a kiss and shouted something unintelligible to her from the famous "sirens" float, decorated with nude statuettes of the mythic sea nymphs who lure mortals to their doom. At the Krewe of Iris parade the next night, she materialized on a different float, this time in bejeweled sunglasses, white evening gloves, and a sequined gown topped with a giant, elaborately beaded collar, her tiara pulsating with multicolored lights as she tossed Deedra a souvenir doubloon stamped with the image of a beautiful long-necked woman. In the French Quarter the following day, she emerged once more, the last in a line of seven or eight women pedaling rusty old bikes up Dauphine Street, all of them wearing pink unitards and purple afro wigs. The cyclist seemed surprised to come upon Deedra there, her bike swerving as she glanced back over her shoulder before vanishing around the corner behind the others.

Then, just when she'd convinced herself that these encounters were more than mere happenstance, they stopped. On Lundi Gras—the day before Fat Tuesday—Deedra wandered for hours among crowds gathered along the riverfront for the annual arrival of the Mardi Gras king but didn't see anyone who looked the least bit like her double. The next morning she was on the streets early for the final day of the celebration but soon saw that she was only deluding herself. What were the odds, after all, that the same stranger had appeared in four different guises in four different parts of town on four different

days, her face always just out of view? True, in all but the first
of these encounters, the woman had seemed to recognize Deedra. But wasn't this, too, a projection? Hadn't that been just
what she'd craved her whole life—to be recognized?

By late morning, she was overcome by an almost physical exhaustion at being in normal clothes amid this vast sea
of masqueraders, an experience that made her feel simultane-
ously hidden and stripped bare. Her AA sponsor had warned
her that sobriety is often accompanied by a profound sense
of loneliness engendered by the loss of friends and behaviors
associated with addiction and that the only way to fight it is
to let yourself grieve your old substance-dependent self. So
maybe it was just time to abandon this ridiculous search, go
home and grieve. Heading back to her apartment, she turned
onto Dumaine Street, where she passed a young woman in a
Cinderella costume who was leaning over and throwing up all
over her slippers. It suddenly occurred to Deedra that despite
being around inebriated people for days on end, she'd never
been tempted to stop for a drink. Not even once. Perhaps this
whole insane chase hadn't been such a waste of time, after all.
As she cut through Louis Armstrong Park, somebody shouted
her name. She turned to see a tall man in a homemade paper-
mache mask that looked like a cruel, smirking baby with
pointed ears. His long, lanky strides felt familiar, and as he
approached, a vivid image of her own brother suddenly shot
into her mind, grinning as he loped over to hand her a gift at
one of her backyard birthday parties in Kalamazoo.

"Do you know who I am?" he asked.

"Not exactly."

"A Billiken," he said, taking off the mask.

It was the boy from her English class.

"I'm guessing you don't know what a Billiken is," he continued. "Few people do anymore, which is a shame. Take the

1940 film *Waterloo Bridge* with Vivian Leigh and Robert Taylor, for example. A Billiken pretty much drives the plot."

He held out the mask with both hands, as if presenting her with a prize.

"Go ahead," he said. "Rub it."

"Is this one of your jokes?"

"No, stupid, it's juju. That's what a Billiken does—bring good luck. It's known as The God of Things as They Ought to Be. By the way, I just saw your doppelganger."

"What? Where?"

Two minutes later she was shoving her way back through the crowd, following the sound of a distant brass band, its song at once mournful and seductive. According to her classmate, the woman in question could now be found wandering around with the St. Anthony Ramblers, a renowned group of locals who held their own informal street parade each Mardi Gras, attracting hundreds of outlandishly costumed marchers. Back in her drinking days, Deedra herself had often taken part in this raucous procession, which made regular stops at local bars as it snaked its way through the French Quarter and the Marigny behind a group of musicians. It was with the Ramblers, in fact, that she'd staggered around in her "ghost writer" getup, stopping random strangers in the street to yell, "You may not know me, motherfucker, but I *created* you!" But this time it was Deedra who was beginning to feel like a character in someone else's narrative. As the peal of horns and rumble of drums grew louder, she pictured her irritating classmate chortling with adolescent glee as he watched her rub his mask and dash off in search of a phantasm he'd created for a fiction of his own invention. And then, at the corner of Burgundy and Touro, she found herself staring at a veiled woman in a white wedding dress, holding an oversized pencil like a wizard's staff. Same shag haircut, same curtain bangs, same heart-shaped face, same embarrassingly wide shoulders and long arms—as the woman made her way through the crowd, using the pencil as a walking stick, she seemed somehow both conspicuous and ethereal, always standing aside, never interacting with the other elaborately attired revelers, who didn't even seem aware of her presence. Deedra couldn't help but think this was all some sort of hallucination, but what did it matter? Was that any reason to stop now? Suddenly, everything seemed imbued with significance, teeming with clues; for the first time, Deedra understood how her parents must have felt as they scoured the beach for signs of their vanished son.

Keeping a safe distance for fear that a face-to-face encounter might break the charm, she vowed that this time, no matter what, she wouldn't lose sight of the woman, who, after splitting away from the St. Anthony Ramblers in Jackson Square, began to lead Deedra on a meandering adventure, sometimes speeding up, sometimes slowing down, sometimes doubling back, sometimes circling an entire block two or three times with no apparent purpose, then rushing forward as if late for an appointment. Hours seemed to blur, and familiar landmarks became unreal. The unoccupied houses, covered with vines; the long-abandoned Municipal Auditorium; the empty skyscraper that was once the Plaza Tower Hotel; the shuttered Market Street Power Plant by the river, its twin smokestacks looming over the pilgrim and her guide—Deedra had never given much thought to these ruins, but suddenly they seemed part of an incomprehensible otherworld that the wanderers were traversing, outside the here and now. Was the ghost writer leading her backward or forward in time? She gave no indication, never even glancing back as she traced a serpentine path through the Lower Garden District and around the fountain in Coliseum Square Park, then to St. Charles Avenue, where the citrusy smell of sweet olive trees hung in the air like a cloud of hashish. Here the ghost writer seemed to speed up, gliding with inexplicable ease over sidewalks strewn with beer cans, plastic cups, and discarded Mardi Gras beads. Polymnia, Euterpe, Terpsichore—in an effort to keep up, Deedra found herself racing across a series of side streets, which, it suddenly occurred to her, were named after the muses, those guiding spirits she'd studied in her Introduction to Classical Mythology course. Melpomene, Thalia—she was sprinting now, weaving wildly through the crowd, then slamming into and nearly knocking over a pair of elderly masqueraders dressed as conjoined twins in an oversized salmon-colored sport coat. Pushing past them without a word, she spotted the ghost writer darting around the corner of Erato Street. By the time Deedra arrived, there was no one in sight.

She stood breathless, terrified that the spell had been shattered. On one side of the street was an upscale apartment complex, its gated parking lot lined with palm trees, on the other a law firm, closed for the holiday, and a restaurant, The Nine Maidens Cafe, to which she now dashed, no ghost writer at the front door (where Deedra saw only her own her own shadowy reflection in the glass), no ghost writer in the lobby (where she squinted into the dark interior of a sleepy tourist spot, the walls lined with posters of oversized fleurs-de-lis and generic jazz musicians and insipid slogans such as "Grooving NOLA-style"), no ghost writer in the bar area or in the dining room or in the women's room or in the men's room (where she barreled in on a surprised patron at the urinal), no ghost writer in the kitchen (where she was cursed at in Spanish by the chef and escorted out by an elfin, unsmiling busboy who, assuming she was drunk, gently led her back to the front of the house). The place was about half full, most of the customers obviously out-of-towners dressed in cheap Mardis Gras T-shirts and other mass-produced accessories. Some were exhausted revelers, thick strings of plastic beads around their necks, dazed looks in their puffy eyes, half-finished hurricane cocktails in their hands. Others appeared to have never started partying or to have given up several days ago, as if they'd come to the café exclusively for the early bird special.

Deedra turned to one of those sober-looking patrons, a woman sitting alone at the bar in front of a cup of coffee, a plate of french fries and an open laptop.

"Did anyone come in here just now?" she asked.

"Not sure," the woman replied, without looking up from her computer.

"She would have been wearing a wedding dress and carrying a giant pencil," Deedra explained, spreading her arms wide to show the size of the object.

"Ah. Well, I probably would've noticed that," the woman said, flashing a sympathetic smile. "So I'm guessing the answer is no."

"I've got to find her," Deedra said, less to the stranger than to herself, a wave of despair overtaking her as she hurried across the room to the front door.

"Good luck with your search."

The voice came from behind her, the calmest voice she'd ever heard.

Pressing her palm against the cool brass of the door handle, Deedra hesitated, then she turned back to the woman at the bar. The face was not animated or exotic, not even beautiful, really. Yet there was something about her, a presence that felt familiar.

"Do we know each other?" Deedra said.

"In my case, that question is more complicated than you might think," the woman replied with an unhurried laugh. "But anything is possible."

In the years to come, when the two women would tell

this story—*their* story, the unlikely tale which brought them together—that last sentence would be the punchline. The assistant coroner would usually start the yarn by recalling that her decision to visit New Orleans had been impulsive and last-minute, brought on by the fact that an elderly aunt was sick with pneumonia. She only happened to be in The Nine Maidens Cafe because it was around the corner from her aunt's house and had good internet. The two lovers would then share an intimate glance before Deedra would launch into the long litany of improbabilities that brought her though the door that day, a tale she often spiced up with details she hadn't considered at the time—the fact that the Mardi Gras parade in which the ghost writer materialized got its name from the patron saint of lost things, for example, or that the street where the ghost writer disappeared and the assistant coroner reappeared was named after the muse of mimic imitation, erotic poetry, and wedding songs. Then, after the women recounted their meeting at the bar and explained what it meant to have face blindness, they'd end with the assistant coroner's punchline, which would often make listeners gasp with delight: *But anything is possible.*

In their telling, it was a story of fate—two people who were destined to be together despite unimaginable odds. Deedra would come to believe that human beings yearn for such narratives—tales of chance meetings and missed connections and unexpected reunions, tales of synchronicities and premonitions and happy endings, presided over by the Billiken, God of Things as They Ought to Be. But Deedra knew that destiny was a lie. She would never mention this, not even to the assistant coroner, but for the rest of her life she would always be standing at that door, studying the woman on the other side of the restaurant. Anything was possible. Perhaps the ghost writer was some sort of supernatural muse who had led her here to meet her future, or perhaps she was a figment of Deedra's imagination, or perhaps she was just some arbitrary person who happened to be wandering around in a meaningless costume, headed for no place in particular. Perhaps Deedra would introduce herself to the woman across the bar, or perhaps she'd simply vanish, just as her brother had, just as her mother had, just as she'd always done, just as all her instincts were screaming out for her to do at that very moment. Turning to the door, she looked for her own reflection in the glass, but the face staring back was still just a shadow, the object of her search once again out of view.

THE PIED PIPER OF FUCKIT

We built the Squirrel Tormenting Device by strapping a lawn sprinkler and hose to a remote-controlled toy truck that Dunnigan had purchased at a yard sale. For the Intermediate Range Ballistic Car Wash, we made a catapult out of PVC pipes, then put it to use lobbing water balloons at Dunnigan's pickup truck in the parking lot behind the closed-down candy factory. The Spousal Warning System was a wireless web cam we hooked up to a tree at the entrance to our subdivision so that we could always know exactly when our wives were arriving home from work.

I was then forty-seven years old; Dunnigan must have been in his mid-fifties. He was the one who came up with the ideas; I sat right down and began sketching plans to turn them into reality. The unemployed editor and the unemployed engineer, right brain, left brain. Under different circumstances, we might have gone into business together, maybe even made a success of it. Instead, we wound up digging the Tunnel.

* * *

Constance and I had bought our place only a few months

before Dunnigan and his wife moved in next door. None of us knew it at the time, but in the previous year, those two houses had been the setting of notorious neighborhood scandal, the husband from my place carrying on with the wife from his. This affair ended loudly, the men swinging baseball bats at each other on the front lawn one morning while children waiting for the school bus screamed in horror. One of the rivals, the story went, ended up in the hospital with a fractured skull, but not before taking out all the windows on his enemy's minivan. I don't know if either marriage survived, just that both couples moved out in a hurry. For months the houses stood empty at the end of the cul-de-sac, matching for-sale signs along empty driveways, lights switching on and off with creepy concurrence, as though hooked up to the same automatic timer. By the time we moved in, the two places had become permanently linked in people's minds, the subject of gossip and curiosity, even derision, as if the structures themselves had done something tawdry and shameful.

I doubt that knowing this chapter of local lore would have stopped Constance and me from buying the place, but there have been times since when, despite my grounding in the rational world of applied physics, I sincerely wondered whether the house was cursed. We bought it after the youngest of our two boys headed off for college, leaving us alone in our previous home, a four-bedroom ranch-style with a garage full of forgotten bicycles and a patio cluttered with skateboard ramps. We told ourselves that we needed to simplify our lives and free up capital for tuition, but I think that old house made us aware of a silence between us, one we hadn't really noticed until the kids were gone. In any case, we barely broke even on the move. Although the new place—a faux arts-and-crafts bungalow—was smaller, it was in one of the most exclusive subdivisions in town, our back yard bordering a thickly wooded forest preserve that gave us a sense of living in the country. We were only the second occupants of the house, its kitchen gleaming with new appliances, its basement still smelling faintly of the carpet showroom, its master bathroom taking up more space than our old den. After years of struggle and sacrifice, Constance and I told ourselves we were finally where we belonged. Seven months after moving in, I lost my job. Then came Dunnigan.

* * *

It did not take long before I realized the man next door was spending most of his time around the house. Not that it surprised me. Within the span of a year and a half, our town in the outermost suburbs of Chicago had lost three of its biggest employers: a pharmaceutical firm that shut down its research facility, a bank that outsourced its call-center operations to India, and the company where I had worked for seventeen years, a maker of medical devices that moved its product-testing division to China. The sight of well-kempt, middle-aged men killing time at the library or tending gardens or pushing carts around the supermarket in middle of the afternoon had become all too familiar. For the most part, we averted our glances and tried to ignore each other.

I had until then only exchanged a few words with my neighbor, a short, round man with hound-dog eyes and a random swirl of thick white hair that seemed to defy whatever attempts, if any, he made to give it order. A tall wooden fence separated his yard from mine, so I knew almost nothing about his comings and goings. But on the bright spring morning that welcomed in the first anniversary of my unemployment, I decided to make myself useful and clean the rain gutters. Climbing the ladder, I heard the sudden growl of a gas motor below me and, turning to investigate, found myself with a clear view of my neighbor's driveway, where an unlikely scene was unfolding.

Dunnigan was fidgeting with a backpack-mounted leaf blower, which weighed down his round shoulders and made him look like a squat, disheveled spaceman. There were no leaves in sight. At his feet were a six-pack of beer, one can already crumpled on the asphalt, and a wooden basket of what appeared to be tomatoes. As the machine roared on, he bent down, cracked open another can, and took a sip. Then, aiming the leaf blower down the driveway with one arm, he grabbed one of the fruits and loaded it into a feeder tube that was duct-taped to the base of the nozzle. The tomato squirted out in a soft arc, skittering onto the asphalt fifteen feet away and rolling to a stop.

Many times since, I have wished that I climbed quietly off that ladder, saving what I had just seen for Constance, an amusing tale to keep the conversation going when she came home from work, tired and tense. Instead, I shouted down to my neighbor. He cut the motor and looked up at me with his jowly face, lips parted in a gap-toothed grin.

"I've just got to ask," I said. "What are you trying to do with that thing?"

"This thing? You, sir, must be referring to the Airzooka."

"The what?"

"A cutting-edge weapons system, my friend. In fact, you have just witnessed its initial field trial," he replied, waddling down the driveway to retrieve the still-intact tomato. "Though let's be frank: delivery to the Pentagon is not imminent."

I found myself laughing, something I hadn't done much of in the recent past.

"Just out of curiosity," I said, "what's the muzzle velocity of that blower?"

"Muzzle velocity?"

"Yes, the mph. The maximum air velocity at the tube."

"Are you suggesting, comrade, that the device lacks proper propulsion?"

"I'm just asking."

"I don't know, to be honest. Do you think it might explain the, er, limited range of my obviously phallic contraption?"

"Could be a lot things. Perhaps your obviously phallic contraption is just too short. Generally speaking, the longer the gun barrel, the higher the velocity."

Dunnigan let loose a happy snuffle. "You, sir" he said, "seem to be a man of considerable technical expertise."

"In a past life, I was a mechanical engineer. Then I went into management. Now I'm what they call redundant."

He tossed off the tomato and hoisted the plastic ring from which dangled the remaining four beers. "Now, now, no self-pity. Come down, friend, and discuss your future. There's a place for you in the fast-growing field of air-powered canonry."

That was how our friendship began. Or perhaps "our jest" would be a better way of putting it, since, other than the inventions, we never had much in common except lack of employment, which we rarely discussed, and laughter. That's what I liked most about Dunnigan—he was always laughing, even when nobody cracked a joke, even when the situation wasn't funny, even when he was full of rage, the same slow, sharp-edged guffaw, har, har, har, like a pickaxe pounding into rock. We spent that first week experimenting with the Airzooka in the forest preserve, where we shot off bushel after bushel of tomatoes, with some kiwifruit thrown in for good measure, until we had the thing more or less perfected. We never told our wives about this or our other efforts, never mentioned the CPKL (Crossbow Powered Kite Launcher) or the FCR (Feline Chariot Races) or the SSPBCBG (Secret Solar-Powered Beer Cooler Behind the Garage). We did not even let them know that we had begun to spend our afternoons together. I was not normally the type of man who kept things from his spouse, and to this day I am unsure why I never told Constance about my adventures with Dunnigan. At the time, I suppose, it seemed pretty simple. If I had revealed that I was wasting my days on a series of private pranks, she would have insisted that I stop. And I didn't want to stop.

* * *

Among the items on our mantelpiece back then was a color photo of Constance and me from the early days of our marriage, a nighttime scene by a lake. I'm looking into the camera, head at a cocky angle, lips fixed in a smirk, a couple of my fingers hooked into the gill of a huge, mud-colored bass, the only fish I've ever caught in my life. Her face, full of summer freckles and shadowed by a wide-brimmed raffia hat, is turned to me in mock adoration. We used to pose a lot like that for pictures— ironic tableaus of a cliché couple in love, doing the things cliché couples in love always do. It's been a very long time since we engaged in such foolishness, but sometimes I think we were never more in love than when we were playacting, never closer than when we were treating marriage as an inside joke. It takes trust to share an inside joke. It takes faith that the other person is your only audience. It takes real intimacy. I have no idea where that picture is now.

I can't say when Constance came to the conclusion that I had stopped looking for a job; perhaps it was before I realized it myself. My severance package had included career transition services with an outplacement company that helped executives and middle managers find work. Its offices were near the hospital where Constance did corporate fundraising, so a couple of days a week I would put on a suit and tie, grab my laptop, and ride in with her. This ritual seemed to give her a sense that nothing much had changed, that the comfortable future we had always envisioned was still out there somewhere. She would flirt with me, hold my hand, talk about the vacations to Italy and Iceland and Australia that we planned to take once things got back to normal.

Things did not get back to normal. The outplacement firm, which occupied the former offices of a failed software company, was supposed to offer us a semblance of our old corporate life, but with its soft lighting and pastel walls and unremitting cheerfulness, it reminded me of the hospice where my father-in-law had spent his final days, coughing up blood. Many of my old colleagues were there, and we tried to keep ourselves busy, calling potential employers and anyone else who might have a job lead, posting résumés on various useless websites, and attending PowerPoint presentations with titles such as "An Optimistic Front is Essential." Nobody was finding work.

I stopped going there even before I met Dunnigan. By then, my severance was about to run out. Constance did not panic; it was not her style. She worked with our financial consultant to free up some cash, took out a new line of credit, and made sure our boys applied for student loans. In normal times, I would have been in charge of such projects, but by now Constance was getting used to making the financial decisions, and I was strangely happy to let her. She had begun to treat me like something of a third son—the grownup deadbeat who mostly gets in the way. Neither of us commented on this.

"Maybe you should look for a part-time job, something to exercise your mind," she said one night as we lay in bed.

"My mind is strong. Never better."

"I'm really starting to worry about you."

"Don't. I'm perfectly content."

"That's what worries me."

The conversation broke off. She was too exhausted to continue, and my head was racing with plans for the Tunnel.

*** *

The idea was simple enough: Dunnigan and I would build an underground passage between my basement and his. It came to us—or rather, to him—one afternoon as we sat around my TV room drinking beer and brainstorming, the outside world flickering past faintly on an all-news channel. We had been looking for something big, a project that would test our intellect and tax our energy, but until that point all our schemes had proved impracticable. I was, in fact, just telling Dunnigan that his idea for a Laser Hedge Trimmer was an unworkable fire hazard, despite its theoretical potential to revolutionize the topiary arts, when he suddenly whirled to the television.

On screen was a grainy video of a thin and irregular passageway, the walls carved from clay, the only light provided by a bare bulb in the low ceiling. This crawlway, we learned, had been used to smuggle Mexican workers into the United States. The reporter closed with a flourish: "No one knows how many people have made this subterranean trek, leaving their past at one end of the tunnel in search of a new start at the other."

Dunnigan switched off the television. Then he darted up and stood over it, staring at the blank screen, fat little fingers combing hurriedly through his white hair.

"Why didn't we think of it before?" he said.

"What? A tunnel?"

He turned to me slowly, his face pink with excitement. "No, my friend, not just a tunnel. An escape."

He began to pace the room, flapping his little arms for emphasis as he talked. "Steve McQueen and James Garner—now, those fellows gave the Nazis a taste of American ingenuity! *Hogan's Heroes*! *The Count of Monte Cristo*! No, my esteemed fellow inmate, these walls cannot hold us. What a lark! Oh, what an epic lark!

But even then I knew that this wasn't just another one of our practical jokes, that it was different in both scale and kind from our earlier efforts. Dunnigan knew it too. He didn't laugh as he formulated the plan; I even detected a hint of menace when he tried to convince me of its merits. I hesitated, aware that I was at the point of no return, that the Tunnel would lead me all the way into Dunnigan's world and away from my own. But a week later, we were purchasing equipment (in cash) from a hardware store a few towns over, where nobody would recognize us. It didn't matter that our "escape" meant leaving one basement for another in the same subdivision. I just wanted out.

* * *

On the day we smashed a hole in the floor of my laundry room with a rented jackhammer, I kept thinking about an unusual antique I'd almost purchased the previous summer in Michigan. Constance and I were then vacationing at her cousin's beach house in South Haven, and one rainy Saturday we decided to go for a drive. After wandering backroads aimlessly for an hour or so, we wound up in one of the bigger nearby towns—Kalamazoo or Portage, maybe Battle Creek—where we saw a sign with directions to an estate sale and, having nothing better to do, decided to stop in.

The item was an old wooden barber pole, or at least that's what it looked like, though the thing was so weathered I didn't even notice the faded red and blue stripes until I held it under a lamp. In my hands, it felt as insubstantial as driftwood.

"That was somebody's little secret," said the estate-sale

agent, a large, chatty woman, with a sticker on her lapel that read "Hello, my name is: THE LIQUIDATOR."

She explained that when she and her employees were preparing for the sale, they'd rolled up a carpet in one of the bedrooms and discovered a hidden trap door cut into the floorboards. "Someone like you probably wouldn't have noticed it—just a few end joints that didn't look quite right—but this line of work, we develop an eye for such things," she said. "Lots of people keep safes and other valuables hidden between floor joists. But this time, the only treasure we found was that whatchamacallit, lovingly entombed in its own velour-lined wooden box. The price, by the way, is one hundred dollars."

When I asked if she had any idea how it got there, the Liquidator shook her head. She didn't know much about the people who'd lived in the house, she explained, other than that they'd seen a lot of unhappiness—somebody supposedly died in an accident, and somebody else supposedly ran away from home and became a drunk, and somebody else supposedly committed suicide. The last one left was the runaway.

"That's who hired me," added the Liquidator. "We did all our business over the phone. She lives in Louisiana now. The neighbors say she came up here not long ago, started a blaze in the backyard, and burned a bunch of family keepsakes and photos until the fire department arrived and told her to stop. When I asked her if she would be here for the sale, she just laughed and said she never wanted to step foot in the place again."

The Liquidator sighed. "People in my profession are librarians of life's tragedies," she said. "More folks than you'd imagine bury their dreams beneath the floor."

Then she added that since I was so interested, she'd be willing to let the pole go for seventy-five dollars. I would have bought it, too, if Constance hadn't entered the room just then to purchase a scarf. At that point, I'd already been unemployed for a few months.

"What would anyone do with such a useless piece of junk?" my wife asked.

I shrugged, but I knew exactly what I would have done with that useless piece of junk. In my mind, I was already prying up the floorboards and placing it back in the dark where it belonged.

* * *

We dug a vertical shaft ten feet deep, shored up the walls with timber and plywood, and threw a pallet on the floor so mud wouldn't accumulate. At the bottom of this pit, we began a horizontal crawlway toward Dunnigan's place. One of us would dig, using a small shovel or mason's brick hammer to chip away at the clay. The other would haul off the loose soil in polyethylene sandbags and stack them on the laundry-room floor, which we had covered with plastic. At the end of the day, we would load the bags out a basement window and dump them in secluded parts of the forest preserve. Then we would clean up the laundry room, put all our equipment in the pit, close the plywood door, and unroll the wall-to-wall carpeting back over the entrance.

I'm pretty certain Constance never found evidence of the Tunnel—which is not to say she was unaware of my attempt to escape. She had been urging marriage counseling—an idea I battled off with procrastination, promises that I would turn over a new leaf—and a prescription for antidepressants, which I quietly stopped taking after the first week. I did not underestimate the pain I caused her, but I could also see that despite my withdrawal, or even because of it, Constance was becoming stronger, more resourceful, and, in some ways, happier, confident in her new responsibilities, liberated from her old bonds of motherhood and home. She had joined a book group, begun making new friends. I knew that she worried about me, of course, and that she missed my income. But she no longer needed me—or at least that is what I had convinced myself.

What went on between Dunnigan and his wife, I will never know. He rarely mentioned her, and I only met the woman a few times. They were an odd couple, I'll say that much. She was four inches taller than her husband and perhaps fifteen years younger, an attractive if unsmiling tax lawyer who did not seem to fit the name Blithe. He told me that they had met while walking their dogs but that after they were married she decided she was allergic to the animals. One day, he came home to find that she had put down not only her own schnauzer but also his beloved golden retriever, Chairman Mao. This had happened five years earlier, but he still had not forgiven her. It took me a few weeks to realize that despite his wicked sense of humor, Dunnigan was a man of fierce grievances, most of them unstated. He mentioned a couple of adult daughters from his first marriage, but when I asked about them, he waved me off. "Goneril and Regan don't speak to the old king anymore," he said. I never learned their real names.

He was only a little less secretive about his newspaper career, which, I came to know, had ended when he took a buyout from his employer of twenty-eight years. I sensed that his departure had been a bitter one and that he missed the job a great deal. But if so, he wasn't talking about it. "I'm past my prime in a profession that's already dead," he declared on that first day of digging. "But what of it? Do our current endeavors not stimulate the mind and delight the senses? The Tunnel—this is our work now."

***

His mood soured dramatically in the second week, which at the time I attributed to our lack of progress. We kept hitting rocks, hunks of bizarrely shaped granite that seemed like three-dimensional Rorschach tests: toasters and teapots and fire hydrants. We had to break them up or pry them out; some were so big we ended up looping the passageway around them. Dunnigan had no patience for any of it. He had grown sullen and irritable, and for the first time since I knew him he made no attempt at gallows humor. I would hear him ahead of me, cursing in the dark, and as I crawled down the shaft to collect another bag of soil, my headlamp would catch his filthy face, eyes gleaming with malice as he hacked away at the earth.

In the beginning, we had regularly traded jobs, but by now Dunnigan did all the shovel work. With his bowling-ball body and a mining helmet perched atop his nest of white hair, he looked like one of the seven dwarfs. He dug with a fury, as if a cavern full of glittering jewels lay just ahead. The air was thin, and Dunnigan stunk to high heaven. We didn't talk. All that existed was the work; everything else dropped away.

On the tenth day, Dunnigan went up to get lunch. Exhausted, I crawled into the passage, stretched myself out on the cold ground, and switched off my headlamp. Darkness smothered everything. Perhaps I fell asleep or perhaps my mind just shut down. Then my cell phone rang. I answered, not thinking how strange it was to receive a signal underground. It was a man from the outplacement company.

"I've been trying to reach you all morning," he said. "You have a job interview tomorrow."

* * *

We had agreed to shore up the tunnel with wooden uprights and crossbeams at four-foot intervals, but this consumed a great deal of time, which Dunnigan now insisted would be better spent digging. When I reminded him of the risks, he just snorted. "Aren't we here to test our mettle? Isn't a bit of danger all part of the jape?"

In the end, he refused to do anything but excavate soil, so I was left to build the bracing myself. It was a two-person job in the best of circumstances, and within a few hours, several yards of unsupported passageway loomed between us. I was on my back, trying to push an upright into place, when I felt the earth give way ahead of me.

Scrambling down the tunnel, I found Dunnigan lying on his side, his head and shoulders buried beneath a heap of clay. It was hard to wedge my way in to help him, and he seemed to fight me, kicking his legs and twisting his fat frame. I burrowed with my hands, pushing away the clods as he gasped for air. We lay inches apart. His eyes were caked shut, and under the glare of my headlamp his clay-covered face looked like a death mask. He spit, licked his lips, drew a deep breath.

"Oh, well, old friend," he said with a laugh. "Back to the mines, as they say."

★ ★ ★

Constance was about to start her morning commute when my cell phone rang. I had been offered the job. She sat down in the middle of the living room floor and sobbed with joy. Somehow this surprised me.

I was worried about how Dunnigan would react, but he took the news with an air of cool resignation, almost as if he'd been expecting it. "Bully for you—a return to life above ground," he said. "The truth is, you've been spending far too much time with the Pied Piper of Fuckit. Sooner or later, the cave door was destined to slam shut."

We divided up the tools and closed the tunnel one last time. It was all very lighthearted, just as it had been on that first day we met. When we shook hands and parted ways, he told me he was going home to cut the grass. I said I doubted that very much. A few minutes later, I heard the sound of a mower on the other side of the fence.

The job was with a subcontractor of my old company. Its salary was significantly lower, its hours longer, its benefits practically nonexistent, its headquarters seventy miles from my house. I was amazed how quickly I readjusted to the rhythm and pace of that world, how easily Constance and I slid back into our old habits—the way she checked my tie every morning to make sure it matched my shirt or the way she sent text messages during the day to find out how some inane meeting had gone. We rarely spoke of the recent past. I did not avoid Dunnigan, but I did not see him, either.

Three weeks after I began the job, we went to dinner at the house of some friends a block away.

"What's that alcoholic neighbor of yours going to do now?" the hostess asked.

"Who?" said Constance. "The short guy next door?"

"Yeah, the one with the pretty wife. She moved out on him."

"Just recently?" I asked.

"No," the woman said. "A month and a half ago. Where have you been?"

* * *

The next time I saw Dunnigan he was standing in the hallway outside my bedroom door, half hidden in shadows. Constance slept next to me in a pair of flannel pajamas. It was four in the morning. He cracked that smirk, and for a moment we just

stared at each other. I can't say I was entirely surprised to find
him there.

He retreated into darkness; I pulled on a bathrobe and followed. I found him sitting in the TV room, a beer in his hand,
his face lit by the all-news channel. He had lost weight, put
on muscle. One of his front teeth was missing. His stench was
indescribable.

"I see you've finished the Tunnel."

"This is just the start," he said, without turning from the
screen. "I'm still digging."

"Why are you here, Dunnigan?"

"Because I want you to see it," he said, turning to me with
bloodshot gray eyes. "Come away, old friend. Come."

"I'm done with all that."

"No, brother. Come see. A quick look."

I followed him to the basement, not understanding why,
not knowing what would happen next. I felt numb. He clam-
bered ahead of me into the hole and soon disappeared around
the first bend, waving for me to follow. I cannot say I wasn't
tempted.

"Dunnigan," I hissed. "Wait."

"Hurry along, friend." The voice already sounded distant,
muffled by the earth.

For a few moments I hesitated, my bare knees pressed into
the cold clay. Then I turned around and scrambled out of the
passage. Back in the basement, I closed the trap door, slid the
washing machine over it, and set to work bolting the thing
shut—by hand, so Constance wouldn't hear.

Later, I stood in the hallway where Dunnigan had stood
so that I could watch my wife sleep. Her skin looked ashen in
the first light, and her face, pressed up against the pillow, was
deeply lined. I could see what time had in store for her. For a
moment, I felt nostalgic for that beautiful young woman in the

picture on the mantelpiece. Then I climbed back into bed and wrapped my arm across her chest.

***

I was on a business trip when the marshals came to Dunnigan's place and piled all his belongings on the front lawn. What amazed everyone in the neighborhood was how little furniture was in that big house. He didn't take any of it, just grabbed some clothes and a few boxes of books and drove off. Nobody has heard anything about him since.

Once again, there are for-sale signs at both houses at the end of the cul-de-sac. During all those months, Constance and I had rarely raised our voices at each other, but after things got back to normal we began to fight. Her rage shouldn't have surprised me, I suppose, but it did. I was stunned when she announced that she was moving out.

I don't think either of us knows what comes next. Constance likes to point out that with the boys at school there's no reason for us to be together unless it's what we really want. I'm trying to convince her that it is. In the meantime, we've moved into separate apartments and put the house up for sale. Neither of us had fond memories of the place.

I waited until my final night there to pour new concrete in that corner of the laundry room. The last time I had poked around down there was that night I bolted the trap door shut. It wasn't my intention to undo those bolts, but I remembered I had left some tools in the shaft. There, I discovered my helmet. The headlamp still worked.

The passage seemed more cramped and serpentine than I remembered, and it felt like a long time before I reached the place where my own work left off. After that, the crawlway became even tighter and less uniform, as if scratched from the earth by some burrowing animal. At times I had to get down on my belly and scoot in a soldier-crawl. There was nothing to shore up the roof: The whole thing could have collapsed at any second, but there wasn't enough room to turn around even if I had wanted to. At last I came to the end of the passage and saw the shaft leading up to Dunnigan's basement. He had left an old ladder against the wall, but when I climbed it, the trap door wouldn't budge. I tried ramming it with my shoulder but almost fell and finally gave up. I was on my hands and knees, about to start the journey back, when I noticed the tiny entrance to a second passageway heading off in another direction. I squeezed inside and crawled along until it forked into two different shafts. Taking the one to the right, I soon came to another fork, and then a third. The air grew thin. I thought I heard noises, steady echoes like thuds of a shovel or gales of laughter, and I found myself hoping that Dunnigan was up ahead somewhere, still searching for a way out. I pushed on, wondering where it would end, but the Tunnel always outstretched the reach of my lamp.

BALM OF LIFE

The ancient twins stood shoulder to shoulder at her doorstep, indistinguishable from each other right down to the matching salmon sport coats, as if in all their years they had never abandoned the habit of dressing alike. Later, she was unable to remember their names, even to recall which one had explained their presence, that they were in town for a seventieth high school reunion, that they wanted to see their boyhood home. They must have mentioned where they now lived, but she could not bring that back, either, just the image of their gray eyes, lusterless as lead slugs, peering past her into the hallway. Had she invited them in? She could not remember it, but how else would they have wound up in her living room, spotted hands clutching glasses of lemonade she herself had poured, bald heads haloed by dust motes in the late afternoon sunlight? She was a hospitable woman, after all, still proud of the house where she had lived for forty-eight years, where she had raised a family, where she had chosen to remain in widowhood, despite her children's urgings to give the old place up. And if she was later to regret the men's visit, she knew that at the time her only misgivings were over unwashed dishes and unpolished furniture. No, she had wanted to show them the house, to let them see the life she and her late husband made for themselves, the kitchen they gutted and remodeled three times, the mantelpiece they stripped down to its original wood, the oak bookshelves they built by hand, now overstuffed with yellowed paperbacks and photos of their children and children's children, the whole clan so spread out these days that they rarely came together under the same roof, even more rarely this roof. Not that she shared such worries with her visitors, leading them from room to room with the practiced cordiality of a tour guide, their impassive eyes studying her from beneath thick white brows as whorled as barbed wire.

She had almost finished taking them through the first floor before it dawned on her that she was the only one talking, that whatever had brought them here, it was not to trade memories of the place. Outside the kitchen, their pace slowed, their eyes shooting from wall to wall as if they had suddenly lost their way. The back staircase, one of them said. What happened to the staircase? She had not expected the accusation in his voice, the anger on his face, and even as she explained how her husband had ripped those stairs out to make room for a second bathroom, even as she regaled them with a funny story about how inept he was as a plumber, how to this day you had to turn on the cold water if you wanted a hot shower and vice versa, she realized those men viewed the renovation as an act of vandalism, saw her as a trespasser in *their* house. She began to wish that they had never knocked on her door, that she was still napping in front of the television, another dull day fading into another dull night. She had been too eager to let them in, she told herself. Was she that desperate for company? She should get out of the house more, meet new people, perhaps do some volunteer work—seventy-three was not that old, after all. Look at these cadaverous pests, still climbing on planes, showing up uninvited at strangers' doors while her life just trickled on like that endlessly running toilet she'd been meaning to fix for years, its serpentine hiss now trailing her down the hallway. Wake alone, bathe alone, eat alone, go to bed alone—it wasn't so bad, really, just as long as you never stopped to think about it, never bothered to wonder if that was all there would ever be—wake alone, bathe alone, eat alone, go to bed alone. No. It had to change. She would stop procrastinating, shake things up, sit right down and come up with a plan the very minute she could get rid of these senile leeches. But for the moment, propriety permitted no escape, not for her and not for them, so she marched her guests back through the dining room, the living room, the front hall, shadows hardening in the dusk.

The brothers panted slowly up the stairs behind her, past restored photos of her late husband's ancestors, unsmiling figures about whom she knew almost nothing but now found herself making up names and stories, here's Great Uncle William who operated a feedlot in South Dakota, there's Cousin Jake who sold Studebakers, embarrassed by these lies yet suddenly determined to deny the newcomers any claim on her walls. The clutter of the second floor surprised her, as if she were suddenly seeing the place through her guest's eyes, the rooms she kept meticulously clean without ever managing to throw anything out, the random pieces of the past—her daughter's jettisoned law school textbooks, her youngest son's trombone, all the items her husband, an inveterate junk collector, had picked up at resale shops and garage sales and farm auctions, a glass ball with the figurine of some monk inside, an autographed headshot of a TV meteorologist, a faded color photo of three men with pompadours, a glass eye, an ivory statuette of a naked little gnome with a pointed head and impish grin, a warped barber shop pole with faded stripes. Where did all these things come from? Where would they go after she was gone? Would they wind up in someone else's house, then someone else's, people only vaguely conscious of their presence, people who couldn't explain their significance any better than she could? Strange to think they had lives of their own, all these objects, lives that would outlast her, and even the house, by decades, maybe centuries, lives as mysterious as those of the strangers across the room, their skin incandescent in the half-light, their sport coats making her think of ushers at the ballpark from when she was a girl, pretzel salt on her tongue and cigar smoke in the air, no thought of it in years, those Sunday doubleheaders with her father, long dead, and her big brother, also dead, the past suddenly so luminous she didn't even need to close her eyes to see it. And now those ushers were taking her by each arm and escorting her down the dark stairway, lifting her off the ground, their strength amazing, their bony fingers dug deep into her skin, and she wondered why she didn't fight them, didn't scream, didn't even look back at the house as they led her out into the twilight. And when she shot out of this daydream, she saw that she was still on the second-floor landing, the twins now staring at something amid the knickknacks on a hallway shelf.

She followed their eyes to a tiny amber bottle, an antique her husband had dug up while gardening. For once the men did not keep up with her as she gestured them toward the stairs but stood gazing at that bottle, one of them whispering inaudibly, the other with a faint grin on his lips, the first time either man had smiled since entering the house. And now the smiling one was clutching the bottle, holding it out for his brother to examine. She rushed to them and snatched it away, flushing at her lack of composure, her unexpected covetousness over some bauble she had all but forgotten, no bigger than the palm of her hand. Tipping it to the lamplight, she noticed how fragile it was, honeycombed with hairline cracks, and then she realized she had never bothered to read the raised lettering: *Dr.*

Gibson's Tonic Elixir / The Balm of Life / Cures Headaches, Rheumatism, All Ills. When she turned back to the brothers, she was surprised to find their eyes meeting hers warmly, as if the bottle had somehow softened their opinion of her. Our mother, said one, used to keep that snake oil in the medicine cabinet. Stunk to high heaven. To high heaven, said the other. Like Turpentine. And then they were laughing, their throats seething, their pale eyes glassy with joy.

Later, after her eldest son had finally convinced her to move into an independent living facility in his town, she often told herself how easy it would have been, and how kind, to let those men have the thing they were seeking, proof that their past was not lost. But in the moment, staring into those faces and listening to that hissing laughter, she squeezed the bottle tight, as if to let it go would be to surrender the whole house. It was not until after the former occupants had teetered back down the stairs and taken their leave that she realized the bottle had broken in her palm—no sound, no blood, no pain, no sensation at all, just a faint glittering of shattered glass in the last light of day.

SONG OF REMEMBRANCE

*Solon of Athens heard his nephew sing a song
of Sappho's over the wine and, since he liked
the song so much, he asked the boy to teach it
to him. When someone asked him why, he said:
"So that I may learn it, then die."*

—*Stobaeus, fifth century* CE

I

At the University of Berlin in the early 1930s, there was a
scholar, now forgotten, who became obsessed with a worm-
eaten piece of papyrus. Fragment 30: that's what he and his fellow classicists called this tattered scrap, which had lain buried
for more than a thousand years in an Egyptian rubbish dump
before being unearthed by British archeologists in 1895. On it
were the last surviving words of an ancient poem, previously
lost to history: μνάσασθαί τινά φαιμι καὶ ἕτερον ἀμμέων.

someone will
remember us I proclaim
in another time

Those lines, the scholar knew, had been attributed to the
Greek poetess Sappho, who, in a transitional epoch between
oral and written storytelling, sang her compositions in public to
the accompaniment of a lyre, the whole performance an incan-
tatory mix of music and magic, evoking in its listeners what the

167

ancients called *thelxis,* or "enchantment." Being a rational man of science, of course, the scholar put no stock in this primitive belief that a song could cast a spell over someone. Nonetheless, he soon found himself slowly falling under the sway of Fragment 30.

Like all his colleagues, he considered Sappho among the most important figures of the classical world. But he also knew that although she'd been praised by countless ancient poets, historians, and philosophers (including Plato, who called her the "tenth muse"), most details of her life, like the missing words of Fragment 30, had vanished. Was she literate? Did she write down the phrase *someone will remember us*—or was it recorded by another scribe, perhaps centuries later? And who, after all, was the *us* in that line? Did Sappho, as some of the scholar's colleagues argued, address her song to a lover, celebrating the timelessness of their shared passion? Was she referring instead, as others suggested, to the musicians and dancers with whom she performed, boasting that their combined genius would survive the ages? Did *us* refer to all women? All women who love other women? All inhabitants of her native island of Lesbos in the Aegean Sea? All Greeks? Did Sappho even compose the song? Or was it possible, as the scholar began to wonder, that it had been on people's tongues long before her birth, long before writing, long before the reach of recorded history, a thing created not by a solitary artist but by a collective fear of being forgotten, a blind horror that eternity might turn out to be nothing more than a shadow we cast on the wall in front of us to prove our own existence, a mirage that vanishes the moment we are gone?

Remember us—he had begun to notice this simple phrase inscribed over and over on artifacts across the ancient world: a Roman cameo (150 CE) from the Anatolian city of Cyzicus, a Phoenician sarcophagus (500 BCE) found near Sidon, an Egyptian funerary stella (2055 BCE) depicting lovers in an eternal embrace, and an Akkadian-language tablet (650 BCE) of the much-older Mesopotamian epic *Gilgamesh*. (*O spirit of Heaven, hear! Remember us, remember!*) Noting that such entreaties often appeared on objects bearing pictures of musicians—the horn player on a Roman mosaic, for example, or the woodwind instrumentalist on a Greek terracotta oil flask—the scholar came to believe in a primeval song of remembrance, sung by thousands of people in thousands of places over thousands of years.

The secret to its survival, he reasoned, must have been an indescribably beautiful melody, so haunting it saturated the listener's whole being, pulsing like blood, and, like blood, passing from generation to generation to generation. Civilizations rose and fell, gods came and went, but the song, he surmised, must still be alive. Like Fragment 30, it was out there, waiting to be rediscovered. And he would make his name by finding it.

Fellow scholars scoffed at the man's theory—an unverifiable hypothesis based on whimsical assumptions and scant data, one of them called it. His closest colleagues urged him to abandon such a dubious new line of research. The profession was crawling with backstabbers, they reminded him, never more than now, when making enemies could cost you your career. Dozens of other members of the faculty had just been purged from the university as political and racial "unreliables." Book burnings were becoming common on the streets of Berlin. And now all university professors were required to take a new oath of loyalty to *Volk* and Fatherland. *Halten Sie sich im Hintergrund,* his fellow classicists urged him. Stay in the background.

He shrugged off these warnings, insisting to his friends that he had no reason to fear. But he knew that this was not true, as his wife often reminded him after tucking their infant daughter into bed. Although she and the scholar had been raised in the Lutheran church of their fathers, their mothers were converts to the faith by marriage, one having grown up as a congregant at the Oranienburger Strasse Synagogue, the other at the Rykestrasse Synagogue. Terrified that this secret might be discovered, she begged him to abandon his frivolous pursuit, or, better yet, to take the family and flee the country, as some of their friends had already done. But where, he replied, would they go? How would they support themselves? He was not, after all, some famous academic who could get a job just anywhere. And besides, what did he have to do with politics or politics with him? The new German Chancellor, that ignorant thug, wouldn't last more than a year or two, he insisted, and until then they must carry on with their lives, just as he must continue his work. On some nights, as the scholar slowly traced the birthmark—shaped like a storm cloud—on his sleeping wife's hip, he imagined himself floating over some isolated village, an airborne figure by Marc Chagall, whom he had once met years ago when the artist lived in Berlin. Somewhere down below, he could feel the song filling the atmosphere, permeating everything, as timeless and sweet as the smell of mountain air. But high above the earth, in a vast bright sky, the scholar found himself entombed in silence.

More and more, he spent his days in the quiet sanctuary of the university archives, poring over photographs of tiny remnants of torn papyrus from that ancient trash heap in the Egyptian town of Oxyrhynchus. These irregularly shaped scraps—which, with their jagged coastlines and jutting peninsulas, seemed like maps of those faraway countries to which his wife always spoke of escaping—were in fact other fragments of Sappho's poetry, many consisting of only a few words. And the longer he studied those puzzling messages from the past, the more he began to think they were meant for him.

Some seemed to offer cryptic clues:

... of a vine / climbing along a / pair of poles ...
... ford at the river ...
... in my dream we conversed, Cyprus-born ...
... all colors mingled together ...

Others were like warnings:

... bringing pain ...
... I'm not sure what to do. I'm of two minds ...
... a desire to die / has a grip on me, / and to see the shores
    of Acheron, / resplendent with lotus and ...
... do not disturb the rubble ...

One fragment contained only a single word:

danger

Outside, the Brownshirts chanted their slogans, the oddly
joyful voices distracting him from his work. He abhorred those
men, of course, but whenever he watched them strut through
the streets, faces full of childlike rapture, he felt a shudder of
recognition at their passion, their sense of destiny, their belief
in being anointed to answer a call from the past. *Someone will
remember us*—he could almost hear Sappho's lovely distant
voice, singling him out as the one who would make her words
come true.

II

In his last moments on earth, the scholar finally succeeded in
consigning his wife's face to oblivion. By then, he had long
since learned to wipe away all that he witnessed the instant

it passed before his eyes. Refusal to recognize—that was how he had survived so long as a *Sonderkommando,* pushing a heavy-laden cart from the gas chamber to the incinerator, then trudging back for another load, hour after hour, day after day. At first, he'd sometimes found solace by imagining himself as Charon, the ferryman of Hades who ushers souls of the newly dead across Styx, river of hate, and Acheron, river of woe. But over time, he taught himself not to think of his cargo as human beings, or even as objects with distinct forms, but only as that which would soon be ash, without attribute or weight. It was best to blot yourself out in the same way, your dreams, your name, even the number tattooed on your forearm, and imagine yourself as residue, shapeless and free, floating up the incinerator's smokestack toward a hazy circle of light. Yet sometimes it was impossible to obliterate the past. Once—a month ago, a year, yesterday?—he had come across the corpse of a woman with a birthmark on her hip in the shape of a storm cloud. He'd tossed it on his cart without looking at the face, but ever since then, he'd been tortured by visions of his wife's pale green eyes, unblinking and unforgiving. It was only the fever that now consumed him, a great fire ripping through his bones and mind, which had finally burned away her gaze.

Disease, starvation, utter exhaustion—it could have been any or all those things. The only question, as he lay shivering on the floor of that cell block, the other prisoners stepping over him without a downward glance, was whether he would die there or in the gas chamber. His ears were ringing now, a faint sound that seemed to come from both deep inside his head and far away. He wondered if his daughter could hear it in England, where, at her mother's insistence, she'd been sent to a safe refuge with strangers. How long ago had that been?

And how old was she now? Eight? Ten? Twenty? It comforted him that, except for a faceless mop of curly brown hair, he'd erased any image of her. For her sake, he hoped she'd done the same with him.

The sound was growing louder now, and more familiar, yet he neither recognized it nor remembered the sweltering day in 1935 when he'd first heard it during a research trip to a remote mountain village in Montenegro. The joy he'd felt at that moment—the unearthly melody, the old man's eyes narrowing as he sang, his bony hands moving over a one-stringed instrument called a *gusle,* the translator whispering those two words—none of it returned to the scholar now. He did not recall how he'd stayed up that night, plying the elderly singer with plum raki and questions, or how he'd returned the next day with his equipment to record the song on an aluminum disc, or how, when he'd played it for his wife back in Berlin, she'd cursed him for risking their lives on a useless old tune, or how, just hours later, he'd heard her humming it as she put their daughter to sleep, or how, listening to her recite that melody, breathy and absentminded, he knew he'd finally found the object of his quest.

There on the rotting floorboards, he gave no thought to the paper he never finished, the notoriety he never achieved, the name he never made for himself. Yet in those last seconds, he finally understood that the noise cascading through his mind was an impossibly beautiful song. He seemed able to pick out the voice of every singer—Sappho, then his wife, then all those he'd carried on his cart, all those who had entered this place and not come out. And at last he, too, joined the chorus, his words vanishing into theirs with seamless harmony, the sound rising up, spreading out, floating away. *Remember us, remember us, remember us,* they sang.

III

The child won't stop crying. The more the woman tries to calm her, the more the infant wails on, her anguished howls churning around that dark room in a whirlpool of panic that builds on itself, engulfing both mother and daughter. The woman's wife has told her many times not to take these outbursts personally. Colicky babies can't help themselves, she says. You only make matters worse when you lose your composure.

If the woman's wife were here, she would instruct her to lay the baby down in the crib, close the door, and do some deep-breathing exercises. Or she'd simply take the child into her own arms, disappear into another room of their suburban Chicago home, then reemerge a few minutes later in a maddening cloud of calm and silence, the infant sound asleep. The woman's wife is—by everyone's estimation, including her own—a natural at motherhood. Just by wrapping the child in her arms, she can quash her hysterics; just by stroking her neck, she can make her feel safe; just by whispering in her ear, she can cause her to twitch with pleasure. It has only recently dawned on the woman that she and the baby respond in almost the same way to her wife's touch.

Cradled in the woman's arms, the child shrieks on and on, twisting and turning and choking down air in great desperate gasps, then shrieking some more. The woman knows that she's holding her too tight to her chest, bouncing her too hard, moving too fast as she paces back and forth in the dark. Her wife has warned her that she could hurt the girl that way. Even so, she can't seem to stop this bitter tango, can't seem to give up on the idea that she's locked in a contest of will, can't seem to tamp down the rage she feels toward the tiny thing in her arms. She will never, she now sees with perfect clarity, be a good mother. No matter how much her wife tries to bolster her, build up her confidence, she will always fail the girl, as if it's her fate, as if it's what all women in her family are destined to do. Her grandmother, a war orphan whose parents died in the Holocaust, raised in a series of foster homes in London and a Jewish youth hostel where the matron beat her until she was deaf in one ear—how could she be expected to love or nurture anyone else? And the woman's own mother, her poor damaged cruel mother, who killed herself five years ago after living for decades in a state of grief since her only son vanished into the Atlantic Ocean while surfing—how could you ask someone who woke up each morning with a fresh sense of loss, someone who marked the anniversary of the disappearance by returning to Florida every year and waiting for her handsome teenage boy to surf in with the tide, flashing his what's-the-worry grin as he toweled himself off, yes, how could you ask someone like that to feel anything but animosity and indifference toward her only surviving child? As the infant's scream drills deep into her sternum, so shrill it seems to come from within, the woman remembers the last time she herself shrieked like that, a long-ago afternoon in New Orleans when she saw a ghost, or not a ghost at all, just someone passing by on the street, a stranger in a yellow sweater who, for reasons she's never understood, reminded her of herself, only somehow more real, more alive, a stranger who kept walking in the other direction. Back and forth, back and forth—in the dark, it's as if she's still chasing after that phantom, or perhaps the phantom is the one chasing her, insubstantial but always there, like a song stuck inside her head. Back and forth, back and forth, back and forth. It does not occur to the woman that she has begun to hum, nor could she name the melody or recall when she learned it. She's only conscious of one thing. Her daughter, now silent, is falling asleep in her arms.

THE REGISTRY OF
FORGOTTEN OBJECTS

Some people theorize the place was built as a storage facility for aeroplanes or dirigibles, machines that, if the old stories are to be believed, once flew above the earth. Others insist it was used for the making of motion pictures, another lost technology, in which human beings somehow transformed themselves into figures of light and danced on giant white walls in front of audiences. Still others postulate it was a temple for some vanished religion. In the end, however, the only thing certain about the building that houses the Registry of Forgotten Objects is that its original purpose has disappeared from history, just like those of the artifacts inside.

Objects made of wood. Objects made of steel, iron, tin, lead, or other metals. Objects made of glass, pottery, or plastic. Objects made of feathers. Objects made of unclassifiable materials. Objects made of pulleys, gears, chains, springs, switches, dials, valves, pumps, and innumerable components that no longer possess a name. Much of the Registry's holdings are from the Mechanical Age and the Electrical Age, but the collection also contains countless artifacts from the Great Forgetting, that cataclysmic period when certain machines, now extinct, are said to have subsumed all human knowledge. The relics that survive—keyboards, screens, and small wafers of semiconductor material—are as mysterious as they are mundane. How these apparatuses worked, and what became of the data they hoarded away, is lost to time.

The Registry is surrounded by nine immense rings of barbed wire, arranged in a spiraling sequence that impels prospective patrons toward the front gate. If it could be seen from above, the long line of applicants for admission would resemble the countless coiled snakes that sun themselves in this arid terrain. The first person in line is a gaunt woman with sunken eyes and a heavy satchel over her shoulder. The second person is an old man cradling a cylindrical object in his arms. Although they've spent many days standing side by side, many nights listening to each other's fitful sleep, the two strangers rarely exchange words, in part because they come from such disparate regions that they do not speak the same dialect, and in part because there is so little to say. Like everyone here, they have the same hope, the same all-consuming dream: entry. Although the man and woman bear no resemblance, their expressions have merged during the long wait into a common look of fatigue, boredom, and intense anticipation—one they share with the third person in line, the fourth, the hundredth, the thousandth, the ten thousandth.

***

The Registry itself, which stretches across this rock-strewn landscape for hundreds of yards, is an arched building of crumbling concrete, shaped like a tube sliced lengthwise in half. At one end rises a great semicircular wall of translucent glass, three hundred feet tall at its highest point, which allows archivists and researchers to work without candles on all but the most overcast days. At the other end—an expansive part of the Registry, off-limits to the public—there's only darkness. Running the length of the building on either side, one hundred feet above ground level, are rows of porthole windows, two lines of dimly lit dots that converge but never connect before they fade into the distance, giving patrons the impression of staring into an infinite tunnel. From the front of the line, the gaunt woman and the old man can make out these endless columns of light through the massive glass doors. Attempting to trace them to their vanishing point, the woman thinks of a future without hunger, fear, or want. The man thinks of a past, stretching on and on behind him before disappearing into that black place where memory begins. He does not measure time in weeks or months or years, concepts he knows nothing about, but in the tired faces of people he has come across in his travels, tired faces like that of the woman in front of him, glimpsed in passing, blurring into one another, nameless figures from some dream. Nothing is solid except the cylindrical object in his arms, which he feels sure is of ancient origin. It alone makes the past seem substantial.

★

Visitors arrive by bicycle, donkey, dogcart, and foot, many of them from hundreds or even thousands of miles away. Some stay for weeks, erecting tents in a cypress grove along the river, the only shady spot in this otherwise barren terrain. These pilgrims generally fall into four categories. The first group comes for practical or commercial reasons: a farmer who hopes to find the function of a rusted piece of machinery, a merchant who plans to make his fortune by discovering a means to reanimate automobiles, a sojourner from the high country who has heard that certain objects might cure her sister's blindness. The second group, self-proclaimed scholars who call themselves the Redeemers, maintain that they can piece together antiquity one object at a time, as if it were a shattered jug. The third group looks not backward but to the days ahead. The Registry attracts innumerable prophets, seers, millenarian visionaries, and their impassioned followers, all of whom believe the place is full of magical fetishes that hold the fate of humankind. The fourth group, which includes the gaunt woman with sunken eyes, are those seeking to become Custodians of the Past—a priestly caste of workers who receive lifetime employment as shelvers and catalogers, and, in turn, must renounce the outside world for a cloistered existence within these walls. Only on rare occasions does a visitor arrive who fits into none of these camps. Such is the case with the old man cradling the cylindrical object, who has come here for reasons beyond his own comprehension, a pilgrim to some innermost shrine.

All who enter must pay a tribute. Some visitors bring rabbit pelts or pouches of candle tallow or foodstuffs (acorns, honey, smoked pigeon breasts, roasted crickets, etc.), but the most frequent form of remittance is an artifact for the collection. Because only the most unusual specimens are accepted, the process often takes hours, even days. Applicants must wait in line under the hot sun as their submissions are examined by a series of officials—Assistant Registrar, Registrar, Executive Registrar, Sub-Archivist, Archivist, Special Archivist for Acquisitions,

Head Archivist for Acquisitions, right up to the Chief Curator, who, it is rumored, oversees the entire operation from a suspended walkway amid the impenetrable shadows high above the great hall.

* * *

Now the gaunt woman with sunken eyes removes the heavy satchel from her shoulder and begins to stack leather-bound volumes on the visitation table. Opposite her, wearing the burgundy robes that signify his rank, the Assistant Registrar eyes those items dismissively. With the exception of certain technical guides, instruction manuals, and other texts thought to contain vital secrets from antiquity, the Registry accepts no books. Almost as quickly as she can place each new volume before him, the man snatches it up, opens it to the title page, snaps it shut, and pushes it aside. Not until the final text, the slimmest of the lot, does he hesitate. Sappho, he says. What is Sappho? The woman shrugs. He opens at random to a page containing only a few words: *do not disturb the rubble.* The Assistant Registrar shakes his head with bemusement. Clearly, this text is of no practical value in deciphering the past. I am sorry to inform you that the Registry is unable to accept your submission, he says with practiced indifference, repeating a phrase he utters hundreds of times a day. Although the woman shows no emotion, her eyes seem to recede, as if she's being drained from within. My journey, she says, took many days. I am hungry. I had hoped to make a new life in this place. The official glances over her shoulder at the next person in line, the old man cradling a cylindrical object. If you'd prefer to leave the books, he replies, you are welcome to do so. The Registry will dispose of them in our pulping vats.

★★★

Because of theft, unruly patrons, and the occasional riot, all Registry officials carry firearms, the function and use of which has never slipped from history. On a recent afternoon, patrons were startled by the echo of gunshots from somewhere within the dark recesses of the building. One rumor has it that an uprising by certain disaffected Custodians of the Past was quickly subdued. But according to a different theory, the shots were fired at (or by) followers of the Erasing Angel, a prophet wildly popular in the countryside, who preaches that each item in the Registry contains the spirit of a dead ancestor. The shaman's followers, according to this version of events, were attempting to bring about the Day of Renewal, when those ghosts take human form and inaugurate a paradise on earth, in which all death, illness, famine, and fear vanish into oblivion.

★★★

Where, asks the Assistant Registrar, did you discover this? By the sea, the old man replies. The official lifts the object, a cylinder of shaped wood, approximately three feet long and six inches in diameter, which seems surprisingly light in his hands. Each end is capped by a sphere of uncertain function. In between, just barely perceptible to the naked eye, twist three helical stripes, one blue, one red, the other white. In his sixteen years of service, the Assistant Registrar has, of course, encountered a number of artifacts that fall into this same general taxonomic category. Not long ago, in fact, a patron presented him with a long, thin pole, atop which was perched a brass likeness of a bird with spread wings (unidentifiable species, presumably extinct). He has not, however, previously encountered a specimen quite like this. And while the object seems unlikely to be of historical importance, the Assistant Registrar has been trained never to make such determinations. All unusual artifacts must be requisitioned and catalogued.

***

It is said that only a small portion of the Registry of Forgotten Objects exists above ground, that the archive stretches for miles in a series of vast subterranean caverns, that these caves, no matter how expansive, fill with objects almost as soon as they can be carved from the earth, and that even now, miles below the surface, hundreds or perhaps thousands of Custodians, specially trained in the techniques of excavating and tunneling, are at work around clock in order to make more room for the past. It is also said that before any object is shelved, it must first be recorded on an endless scroll of paper that moves in only one direction, like time itself.

***

The Assistant Registrar places the cylindrical object on one pan of a scale then puts several stone discs on the other pan until the rusted metal beam between the two sides is level. What are you doing, asks the old man, who has never seen a scale before. The bureaucrat scribbles some numbers in a little book, then takes out a caliper, opens its jaws until they encompass both ends of the item, makes a few adjustments, and jots down several additional notes. Finally, he turns to the old man, and, with an air of condescension, replies, I am measuring your object so that perhaps we might one day determine its function. The old man, who cannot read words or count to twenty, has no desire to argue with such an eminent official. Nonetheless, he is quite sure that the importance of this artifact has nothing to do with its weight or its length but with its stripes, which, he has discovered, contain a kind of magic. If he holds the cylinder upright and spins it, those stripes seem to rise and rise and rise and rise. Surely, he thinks, this must be the object's purpose—to be lovely and to give a person hope. Isn't that why he came all this way with the relic, to ensure that something beautiful would not be lost? Suddenly, he wants to tell the other man about his life, the life of a wanderer: the time he fell off a roof (the scent of a lilac bush that broke his fall), the time he awoke to find his wife and child gone forever (the lingering smoke of the previous night's campfire), the time he saw a flock of pigeons so dense it blocked the sun (the abrupt nightfall, the chill, the rustling of wings like a distant sea), the time two strangers invited him to their shanty for turtle stew (the sour flavor, the warmth of the bowl, the hunger easing, the gratitude). None of these experiences overlap, none of his stories connect, and yet somehow, he thinks, they are all of one piece. That's what he wants to say: that everything is intertwined like those stripes, everything is part of a pattern, everything rises. But it's too late. Without a word, the Assistant Registrar has begun to bear the object away, fading into those lightless regions where only the elect may travel.

ACKNOWLEDGMENTS

For its author, this book itself has sometimes felt like a forgotten object—one that easily could have remained hidden. I'm grateful to those who helped to bring it out of the shadows, not least Lee Martin, the judge of the 2023 *The Journal* Non/Fiction Award, and Kristen Elias Rowley, the editor-in-chief of The Ohio State University Press, as well as the talented team at Mad Creek Books, including Tara Cyphers, Zachary Meyer, Nathan Putens, Samara Rafert, Olivia Sergent, and Juliet Williams.

I also wish to express my thanks to the editors of the following publications, where the stories in this collection first appeared: "The Drought" and "The Man Who Slept with Eudora Welty" in *Ploughshares*; "Beachcombers in Doggerland" in *The Sun*; "Postcard from a Funeral, Cumberland, Maryland, October 10, 1975," in *Mid-American Review*; "The Complete Miracles of St. Anthony: Definitive Edition with Previously Unpublished Material," in *Conjunctions*; "The Master of Patina" and "The Pied Piper of Fuckit" in *AGNI;* "Why I Married My Wife" in *Michigan Quarterly Review*; "Four Faces" in *failbetter*; "Balm of Life" in *Fiction* (published as "The Former Occupants"); "Song of Remembrance" in *Chicago Quarterly Review*; and "The Registry of Forgotten Objects" in *North American Review*.

The epigraph at the beginning of this book is from Wisława Szymborska's "Still Life with a Balloon," translated by Stanisław Barańczak and Clare Cavanagh, and published in *Poems New and Collected: 1957–1997* (Harcourt, 1998). The Sappho quotes are adapted from the following books: Anne Carson's *If Not, Winter: Fragments of Sappho* (Vintage, 2002), Guy Davenport's *Sappho: Poems and Fragments* (University of Michigan Press, 1965), and Suzy Q. Gordon's *The Poems of Sappho* (Library of Liberal Arts / Bobbs-Merrill, 1967). Some Sappho aficionados will perhaps protest that a fragment frequently quoted in "Song of Remembrance" (*someone will / remember us I proclaim / in another time*) was not, in fact, discovered in an Egyptian rubbish heap in 1895, as the story indicates, but came from different source. I plead guilty to being what Sappho called μυθόπλοκος, a weaver of fictions.

Several illustrations in "The Miracles of St. Anthony" are from Thomas F. Ward's *Saint Anthony: The Saint of the Whole World* (Benziger Brothers, 1898). The other images in that story are the digital creations of Azize Altay Harvey. I'm grateful for her talent, time, and patience, and I'm delighted by the opportunity to collaborate with this gifted graphic artist.

I owe a huge debt of gratitude to my agent, Sloan Harris, for his support in good times and bad. The same can be said for Richard Cohen, as well as for all those who have tasted the Wine of the Millenium. Abiding thanks and love also go to my brother, Matthew "Best I Got" Harvey, and to the other patrons of the back room at Tom's Blatz. Praise is further due to the devout elders of the Holy Church of Al & Andy. Additionally, I want to offer a heartfelt note of appreciation to my talented and supportive colleagues at DePaul University, especially the faculty and staff of the Department of English, as well as Mary Devona Stark, Senior Associate General Counsel at the school, for her much-appreciated legal wisdom. Gigantic thanks, as well, to Sheryl Johnston, a wonderful publicist and friend.

I'm grateful to Randy Bates and James Murphy, who perused sections of this book for factual accuracy. I was blessed with other insightful readers as well, including Scott Blackwood, Bill Lychack, Mike Paterniti, Cammie McGovern, Tom Henry, and the members of my writers' group (Doro Boehme, Maria Finitzo, Ann Goethals, Peter Handler, Laura Jones, Gwen Macsai, Francesca Royster, Gail Louise Siegel, and Andrew White), many of whom have read many drafts of these stories over the course of many years. Special thanks to Lauren Cowen, a good friend and brilliant editorial mind, whose input was crucial to the completion of this project.

Finally and forever, to Azize and Julian, thanks for turning out to be such spectacular, smart, and complex human beings. And to Rengin Altay, thanks for all these years, all this joy, and all the journeys that lie ahead.

THE JOURNAL NON/FICTION PRIZE
(formerly The Ohio State University Prize in Short Fiction)

9 780814 259146